I0589307

CON JOB

Laura VanArendonk Baugh

Æclipse Press
Indianapolis, IN

Text copyright 2014 Laura VanArendonk Baugh

Cover illustration & design
copyright 2014 Kristie Good, Crash Bang Labs

ISBN 978-0-9859349-7-2
www.Aeclipse-Press.com

All rights reserved. This book or any portion thereof may
not be reproduced or used in any manner whatsoever
without the express written permission of the publisher,
except for the use of brief quotations as in a book review.

For all the geeks.

Nerd on, my people.

Author's Note

Fan conventions come in many flavors. There are conventions dedicated wholly to a medium, such as anime or comics or tabletop games, or to a subset of media, such as BBC television, or to a specific title or franchise, such as *Star Wars* or *My Little Pony* or the various incarnations of Sherlock Holmes, or to a genre, such as science-fiction or mystery. They can vary widely not only in content but in feel. How welcome are other fandoms at this particular convention, or should you wear your *Assassin's Creed* shirt at a sci-fi con? What regional idiosyncrasies will set this fan gathering apart from one on the opposite side of the country?

What will the people be like? A small sci-fi con might feel quite insular, while an anime con of the same size will probably include group dancing in the corridors to music someone is DJing from a corner, with plenty of enthusiasm and even hugs for a passing cosplayer dressed as a favorite character. (Always ask first! Not only for personal space reasons, but for care of the costume as well.) Some conventions limit the number of attendees, cutting off registration at a certain point, while others welcome all comers. Some are run with steampunk-clockwork precision, while others are very... loose. Some call the judging and display of costumes a masquerade, others a fashion show, others just a costume contest. At small cons without a lot of cosplay emphasis, costumes may be judged with only a glance on the stage, while at other cons judges may spend two full days examining the entries individually before they finally all go onstage.

While some of these differences can seem divisive or confusing (I have seen a con attendee stumped by the lack of a "vendors' hall," while not knowing what the "dealers' room" was), in the end cons all share the same general feel. A group of otherwise-unconnected people have come together to celebrate something they enjoy in common. It's not a phenomenon which occurs frequently elsewhere; they haven't come just to spectate or be entertained, as at a playhouse or cinema, they haven't come just to buy or sell, as at a specialty store, and they haven't come just to accomplish, as at a race or sporting event. They've come to share their enthusiasm with other enthusiasts.

Come and join the enthusiasts and fans at Con Job.

Special thanks to Sandy Della-Croce, Kate Allen, TR Goodman, Nancy VanArendonk, Dave Heigl, and Jennifer Bak for a delightful and hilarious discussion of fandom-themed food puns. I am only sorry I could not include more at the — ahem — Admiral Snackbar.

Chapter One

"What do you mean, it's not there?"

The registration girl shook her head. "Could it be under another name?"

Jacob reached for his back pocket, glad he'd had the foresight to print his receipt. "Jacob Foster, see? Three-day badge."

She shook her head. Beside them, the next line shuffled forward as attendees claimed their badges. "No, that's just your payment name, it won't be under that. Lots of people buy badges for friends or kids. Your badge name is entered separately. But at least we know you should have one. Can I see that?"

He passed her the receipt, and she copied the address into the computer. She frowned at the screen as a few more attendees beside them collected badges and headed off into the convention.

Jacob glanced to his right, where Sam waited. She was trying to be patient, but she had her own badge already clipped to her jeweled belt. She was tapping at her phone, probably explaining they were delayed.

"Man, what's up with these lines?" grumbled someone behind him.

"It wasn't like this last year," said someone else. "This is crazy."

"Ah, here you are," said the registration girl, bending to look at the screen. "Instead of your name, it just shows your email address."

"What?" Jacob tried to lean forward and see the screen, but the angle was bad. "I wouldn't have done that."

"Well, it's here." She shifted her eyes toward him as she started the label printer. "Though to be fair, you might not have. All pre-reg badges were entered by hand; someone might have done the entry wrong."

Jacob stared at her, seeking a way to ask the obvious question without sounding as if he were blaming her personally. "There's eight thousand people coming here, and the registration is done by hand? After all the info was entered online?"

"I know, I know. Rita, that's the reg DH, she really wants to use one of those online ticket systems, you know? But con chair doesn't want to." She hesitated and then crumpled the freshly printed label instead of applying it to the plastic badge. "Sorry, it's got your email as your badge name. Let me change this and print something else for you. I mean, it's probably not as bad if you were a girl, but you know…."

"No, I appreciate it." And another minute longer wouldn't hurt at this point.

The printer spat out another small adhesive label, and she smoothed it onto the brightly-colored badge. It now read *Jacob Foster* instead of the screen name he normally used, but it was an improvement over *TheShinyNewJacob@gmail.com*.

She handed him the badge. "Badge holders, lanyards, and program books are to your right. Have a great con."

Samantha looked up as he joined her. "You ready?"

They moved around a pack of blood-soaked, ravaged half-men — survival horror was big this year — and slid past the growing registration lines. Jessica and Zach were waiting where the hotel ballroom opened into the corridor. "Hey!"

Zach jumped up, trailing a floor-length scarf. "I thought you'd be in line forever."

"Careful!" Sam blocked his greeting hug with one arm and an apologetic smile. "I ran out of silicone rubber, so a couple of these armor spikes are resin, and they won't flex when you hit them."

"Right in the solar plexus," Zach observed. "Death by cosplay."

"A fitting end to anyone who touches a costume without permission," Jessica pronounced. "But you made it!" She stood, her *Twilight Princess* Zelda costume making her look taller than her natural petite stature. "Registration still that bad?"

"Ridiculously slow," Jacob said. "Did you know they're entering everything by hand? I wanted to check a calendar, see if we were back in the nineties or something."

"I know! People are complaining all over Twitter. But I guess it'll get better as people get in, right?"

Jacob wasn't in costume, so he got a full hug. "Good to see you," Zach said. "Guess who I am?"

Jacob looked at the scarf. "The Fourth Doctor?"

"Normally, you'd be right. But me, I'm Doctor Hu. Get it?"

"Zach, quit," Jessica said. "That's totally racist."

Zach tapped his face. "I'm Asian. And my name is Hu."

"Still racist," she said. "Racist is racist regardless of who you are."

"*Who* you are?"

"Tell him he's not funny," Jessica said to Jacob. "And hi, by the way."

"Hi. Seen Sergio around?"

"Not yet. But his panel's today, so he might be setting up or something."

Zach opened his program book. "Anybody know where the signings are? Last year they were in the back of the vendor hall, but that was crazy crowded, so I hope they moved them."

"Which one do you want?"

Zach found the list of guests and ran his finger down, looking for autograph info. "Mickey Groene, Sandra Shark — I swear that's a fake name, I don't care what she says — Ryan Brazil, Andrew Freeman, Tiffani Snyder…. Here you go, Jacob, Greg Hammer."

Sam leaned over his shoulder. "One two-hour slot? And he's here only for his panel and the signing? That's going to be packed."

"Well, it's the only one I care about, so I'll be there." Jacob reached into his backpack. "I brought my first edition *How to Die* to get signed."

"Cool!" Zach took the book and held it carefully, admiring the stark block typography, *How to Die In Five Easy Steps*. "Wow, great condition."

"I try." Jacob took it back and slid it into the inner pocket of his bag again. "You guys ready? Let's hit the vendor hall. It should have just opened."

The vendor hall was only a few corridors away, but it took longer to reach because every few steps someone stopped them to ask for a photo of one or all of the costumes. Jacob held their bags as Sam, Jessica, and Zach fell into various practiced poses with each request, exchanging mutual thanks with the photographers before moving a bit further.

Finally the group held up or pointed out their badges to the staffer at the entrance and then headed inside the joined ballrooms which formed the dealers' room. The hall was already filling with attendees eager to shop for comics, figures, DVDs, posters, books, charms, jewelry, art, and more.

"Who's Megan?"

"What?" asked Jacob.

Zach pointed. "Who's Megan?"

Jacob followed his gesture and saw an enormous banner reading "MEGAN!ME" suspended over an open booth several times the size of the vendors on either side. "Not Megan, Meg-anime. It's a pun, or it's trying to be one but is bad at it. Kind of like you."

"I don't follow anime."

"It's a big company which just bought up a couple other company catalogs, making a lot of waves. People aren't sure if it's a good thing because maybe more titles will get released over here, or if it's bad because they ate up competition and will raise prices. Too early to tell where they're going. And they got some fan favorites, too." Jacob started toward the booth.

Sam was right beside him. "They've got *Season of the Dove*, and I haven't been able to complete my set since they bought out Famion last year. I just need two more discs." She gave him an embarrassed smile. "I know, but I want all the DVDs. They have this really cool image on the spines, forming the Final Seal the Spellknights use…. It looks cool, okay?"

Jacob held up his hands. "Am I arguing?"

They reached the table, and Samantha began scanning the DVDs. Jacob browsed beside her. He wasn't looking for anything in particular, but he wouldn't mind finding a copy of *Ice War*, or a figure set….

"Here it is!" Samantha beckoned to one of the sales staff and pulled first one DVD, then another from the bin. She drew cash from the concealed pocket in her jeweled belt and flipped the DVDs over. "I'll take both of — wait." She flipped the boxes again. "What happened to the covers? Where's the seal?"

"Nice Spellknight costume," commented the salesman. "You want both of those?"

"I want these volumes, but with the Final Seal artwork," Sam said. "Where are they?"

He shook his head. "Those are the only ones."

"Can I order the others?"

"No, there aren't any others. That's the only version released."

Sam looked at him. "That's not true. Famion had the complete set with the Final Seal artwork."

"Those were recalled and destroyed. This is the MEGAN!ME release."

Sam stared. "Destroyed? They destroyed the Final Seal art versions?" Her jaw worked a moment. "That was *why* I bought the DVDs. I could have bought the series digitally for cheaper, but I wanted the Final Seal art. I skimped on rehearsals to work extra hours to get them. The whole reason people were buying the DVDs, and you trashed them?"

"They had the Famion logo." He pointed to the discs. "These have a new special feature, a fifteen-minute interview with the CEO of MEGAN!ME about the anime market—"

"I don't want an interview with some suit instead of the art that would complete my set!" Sam looked down at the discs again. "And — wait, is this the real price? That's ten bucks more than the Final Seal art version!"

The salesman had the grace to look sheepish. "Well, the company took a loss in destroying the other stock. And this one has an extra feature, that interview."

Sam slapped the DVDs down on the box of discs. "I think I'll pass, thanks."

He nodded, almost apologetically. "If you want to say

anything," he said, dropping his voice, "there's a VP here. Just today and tomorrow." He nodded toward the far end of the booth, where a petite woman in a dark blue power suit was shoving a program book into a man's chest. Sam glanced at her and then back at the man, and one corner of his mouth crooked upward. "I used to do marketing for Famion. Now I'm working the exhibit hall booth."

Sam nodded once. "Thanks." She started toward the far end of the booth, and Jacob went with her.

"Look at it!" the petite woman snarled, pointing at a page in the program book. "It's wrong. Totally wrong. If you're not even going to get our name right, then I'm pulling our sponsorship right now. We will walk, and you'll owe everything we gave you."

"Wait, look," said the man. "You can still read it. It still says mega-anime."

"It's MEGAN!ME," snapped the woman, "and the exclamation point is missing. That's an I."

"People are still going to know exactly what company it is."

"That's not the point! Branding is very important. I want this fixed!"

"There are thousands of program books already distributed," he said with an incredulous little squeak. "Even if I could somehow have thousands more printed in the next couple of hours — which is impossible…." The man trailed off as he noticed Sam and Jacob, and he seemed to deflate a little. "Look, if you guys have a question, can you take it to Con Ops, please? I'm kind of tied up at the moment."

"Actually, we were waiting to talk to you," Sam said, looking at the woman in the suit.

She gave them a frigid look. "Are you sure you have the right person? I'm not con staff."

Jacob caught Samantha's arm. "We can see you're busy," he said. "Maybe later."

Samantha pulled away. "I'd like to give you some customer feedback."

"Feel free to talk to the guy behind the table."

"He suggested I speak with you—"

"Sorry!" Jacob cut in. "We'll talk with him and maybe try to catch you later."

Samantha went with him, scowling. "What a hag," she said. "Why'd you stop me?"

"I read the face of that guy she had by the throat. Anything we said was going to be his fault, you know?"

"You might be right. Poor guy. Did you hear her? Yanking their sponsorship because of the letter I?"

"It's *supposed* to be an *exclamation point*."

Sam laughed. "I'll bet she made the Final Seal art decision herself," she said. "Personally. With the artists pleading and crying in front of her desk, holding photos of their starving little kids. And puppies."

"Real puppies, or pictures of puppies?"

"Both."

Zach and Jessica were still browsing the dealers, so Jacob and Samantha started for the door on their own. The room was getting crowded, and Sam preferred to avoid crowds. As they passed a booth of fan art Jacob turned to examine a Wonder Woman poster, and bumped into someone. "Sorry!"

"No problem," said the young woman, smoothing a

strand of hair back into place. She wore a neat blue business suit with a corsage, and her convention badge hung behind a more traditional industry badge which read, *Hello, my name is Laura.* "All good."

Sam frowned as they went on. "She's got to be in costume, with that badge, but I can't place it."

"You can't recognize everyone, not at a mixed con like this. Too many fandoms."

"No, this is something I know. It'll come to me in the middle of the night or something."

They passed the row of video rooms, mostly empty this early in the convention. Jacob slowed to read down the schedule of the first, hoping against reason that *Ice War* would be on it. No such luck; the room was presently screening season two of *Battlestar Galactica.*

"Jacob."

He glanced up, caught by Samantha's tone. She was standing outside the door of the second room, looking inside, and as he watched her eyes shifted to catch his.

He took a few steps to join her and looked in at the enormous screen which should have been, per the schedule posted on the easel outside, showing the Tenth Doctor. Instead, a fat woman and a chubby, bleached-blond little boy were screaming at one another.

Jacob's stomach clenched and for a moment he couldn't breathe.

On the screen, the little boy turned and yanked down his elastic-waist pants, mooning the shouting woman with barely-pixelated buttocks.

Jacob crossed the empty room to the DVD player and slapped the eject button. The disc which came out wasn't commercial, just someone's home-burned copy with permanent marker spelling out *Cougars and Cold Ones.* Jacob snapped the DVD in half and threw the pieces into the trash can in the corner.

"Right," Sam said. "No telling where that came from. Somebody's idea of a practical joke." She took a breath. "We going to Sergio's panel?"

Chapter Two

Sergio's session was supposed to be on the import and translation process to bring foreign media to the US, but judging from the abandoned slide about distribution channels on the over-sized wall screen, the discussion had gone its own way. Samantha flipped a little wave at Sergio as they took seats in the back, but he didn't seem to see them. The room wasn't large, but it was nearly full.

"The point is," a guy in a printed Mr. Spock t-shirt said, "you don't own the rights. We don't own the rights. It's the creators' call, and if they don't want to share a show, they don't have to."

"I totally agree with you about creators' rights," Sergio said, his voice terse, "absolutely, but the problem is, it's not always the creators who are making that call."

"But—"

"Let me use an example," Sergio interrupted. "Let's take *Mr. Doobles* as a case study. Has everyone heard of *Mr. Doobles*? It's a cute little Japanese show about a bunch of kids who draw stories together, has a cult fandom probably beyond what it deserves, though I could get flamed in some circles for that. It was licensed for the US by Pop Culture, but when they started having money problems a few years ago they shelved most of their family-friendly stuff and bet on the *Death March* franchise to save them. Sound familiar, you with me? Well, it didn't work, they went under, and last year MEGAN!ME acquired the Pop Culture catalog, including *Mr.*

Doobles."

Heads bobbed around the room; a lot of the audience knew this story.

"So internet explosion, hooray, *Mr. Doobles* is going to be released again! Because Pop Culture had been a few years behind the overseas releases and everyone wanted what they'd been missing. But MEGAN!ME didn't release anything."

"Here he goes," murmured Sam with a suppressed smile.

"You tell 'em, Sergio," Jacob whispered back.

"In fact, not only did they not release any of the backlogged *Mr. Doobles*, they put out a statement saying they had no plans to release any new *Mr. Doobles* material in the foreseeable future. But then they started issuing cease-and-desist letters to fans who were translating scripts of overseas releases."

"Yeah!" called someone from the front rows. "Like that show about the radio station, where they lied about the fan mail so they could cancel the show even though it was really popular."

"Or like *Firefly* got scuttled, though at least it got a DVD release."

Sergio nodded. "And MEGAN!ME isn't making any money on *Mr. Doobles*, either, which means fans won't get anything like it in the future and more creators won't get picked up. So the TLDR is, some stuffy hateful exec kills a series, maybe just because of some personal reason, and everyone — fans, creators, everyone — gets screwed."

The room exploded into agreeing applause.

Sergio pointed at the screen, probably referencing a slide which had been visible earlier. "I don't like piracy. I have friends who are artists and writers, and I want them to get paid for their work. But rule number one of marketing is, Make it easy for people to give you their money, and right now it is legally *impossible* to give anyone money for *Mr. Doobles*. Honestly, getting the license dropped would be the best thing for *Mr. Doobles*, because then maybe some other company could pick it up and actually sell it to the people who want it."

More cheers and whistles. The guy who had protested earlier said something, but Jacob couldn't hear it over the audience's agreeing with Sergio.

But Sergio had heard, and he shook his head. "That's good in theory, but you know it's not the only factor. You think there are no human personalities in the industry? No one ever gets a bee up his nose or a stick up his butt about a certain show or creator or whatever? And like he brought up about that radio show, if you can feed bad info to the board you can get whatever decision you want, maybe even get yourself a nice bonus for making them think you're saving the company money. No, market demand is a big part of it, sure, but it's not everything."

Someone stood and called, "So what do we do about it? You're totally right — writing to MEGAN!ME doesn't do anything, those letters don't get passed on to the suits. And it's not like the board of directors is actually reading all this on Twitter or Tumblr or anything. So what do we do?"

Sergio grinned. "We find an exec, we slap him around until he's willing to listen, we tell him to shut up and take our money, and if he isn't cooperative we push him into a busy highway." He laughed and shook his head. "Seriously, man, I don't know. That's the thing, we're just screwed. They're the gatekeepers, and as long as we have this stupid licensing system that makes it illegal to buy direct, we just have to wait for them to die off. Pop Culture did already; maybe MEGAN!ME will be next. We can only hope."

Someone beside the door signaled, and Sergio nodded. "Right, sorry, that's time. Gotta tear down and get out for the next panel. Thanks for the talk, everyone!"

"There's a petition online about *Mr. Doobles....*" someone shouted over the shuffle of the audience rising and starting toward the door. Jacob and Samantha went along with the river of exiting attendees and then slid into an eddy beside the door.

A few minutes later, Sergio came out, carrying a tablet and adapter. "Hey, guys! Good to see you!"

"You too. Got a bit exciting in there?"

"The Con Job crowd's always a little more interested in the business side of things. That's why I can even do an import and distribution talk here; wouldn't fly at a lot of cons. You guys got dinner plans?"

"Probably getting pizzas in the room. I'll text you when we're thinking about ordering."

"Sounds good."

Samantha snapped her fingers and pointed at a woman passing in the hall. "You! I'm sorry, I've been trying to think since I first saw you. Who are you playing?"

The young woman in the blue suit fingered her *Hello, my name is Laura* badge. "To be fair, most people don't remember the blue suit, and it's from a book, so there wasn't a really clear visual...."

Jacob noticed her slicked hair was now a bit fuzzy, her corsage had been crushed, and she seemed to have rubbed her suit against something dusty. "You okay? I didn't do that, did I?"

She shook her head. "Oh, no. I'm going to look just a bit

more bedraggled each time you see me, because—"

"Because you're decaying!" Sam clapped her hands together and pointed. "You're dead Laura, from *American Gods*!"

"Yes!" Dead-Laura was clearly delighted to be recognized. "I'm doing her all weekend, and each time you see me I should look just a little more dead." She popped open the small bag she carried to show a wallet, a squeeze bottle of some particulate, and an eyeshadow palette in greys and browns. "I figured most people wouldn't get it, but I've always wanted to do it."

"I think it's brilliant," Sam said.

"And you? Who are you?"

Sam looked down at her costume. "Sister Rostia, from *Season of the Dove*. This is her first outfit, but I really want to do the Spellknight Arcane version as soon as I get some help sculpting for the armor resin casts—"

"That's enough," Sergio said, holding up his hands. "In a minute she'll be talking about wig wefts and Worbla, and I'm outta here before we get to that point. See you guys later."

"You're just self-conscious about your lame black t-shirt!" Sam called after him, smiling. She looked at Dead-Laura. "He doesn't really appreciate costumes. What a poser." Her grin belied the taunt.

"Are you really working with resin and Worbla? Can I ask you some questions about it? I just tried my first armor piece last week, and — well, I guess the tutorial I found left out a couple of steps I was supposed to know about."

"Sure! I'm not much of an expert, but I'll tell you what I can, and I can point you toward some really good tutorials."

"That'd be great, thanks!" Dead-Laura drew out her phone. "How'd you like me to contact you?"

Sam thumbed her phone. "What's your number? I'll

text you to join us for dinner, if you want. We typically all chip in for pizza, and there will be a lot of costume nerds."

"Perfect! I'm CosBright." She looked a little embarrassed. "It's sort of a dumb name, but I started posting back when I first wanted to go to cons, and now too many people know me by that to change it."

"Oh, I understand that." They exchanged numbers. "It'll be around nine or so, if that's okay. Brittany and Andrew have to finish their costuming panel first."

"Brittany and Andrew? Like, Fish Face Costumes, with all that amazing leatherwork and beading?" CosBright's eyes were wide. "Oh, I will so be there."

Jacob's phone buzzed with an incoming text. *Hey, could you volunteer a few hours with security? We had a couple of no-shows, various reasons, and I said you'd be a good guy.*

Jacob typed a reply. *Sure, if you can schedule me around the Greg Hammer signing. My one goal this weekend is to see him and get an autograph.*

I can probably swing it so you're his security. That work for you?

It certainly did.

Dead-Laura had moved on, and Sam was flipping through the con's mobile app. "What next? There's a panel on gender roles in sci-fi, and one on building magic systems for games and fiction, and one on hobbit genealogy."

"As much as hobbit genealogy intrigues me, I just said I'd check in and do some security shifts for the con. Daniel texted me, said some of their staff didn't make it."

"Does that mean that you can tag my Glaive of Truth tomorrow even if it measures a quarter-inch over hall limit?"

"We'll see how nice you are to me."

Chapter Three

Daniel had mocha skin, stood six feet even, and showed every one of his forty-two years. He looked good in an Imperial officer's uniform from *Star Wars*, but he ruined the effect by grinning and waving as Jacob entered. "Hey, Jacob! Thanks, man."

"No problem, glad to help."

Daniel gestured to catch the attention of another man at a table with an energy drink. "Vince, this is Jacob. He's going to help fill the gaps. I know him from the Academy."

Vince was the man who had been trying to placate the angry MEGAN!ME executive, Jacob recognized. "Glad you can help us out," Vince said, extending a hand over the table. "You a cop too?" He didn't seem to remember Jacob, which was fine by Jacob.

"Not yet," Jacob said. "Hope to get into the Academy soon. Actually, security will look good on my application next month."

"Con Aid," corrected Vince. "Can't say 'security,' gives us liability issues."

Daniel kicked a plastic tote toward Jacob. "Rummage through that and find a shirt your size."

"Excuse me." A teenager in improbable armor leaned through the pass-through desk cut into the wall. "Can we get our props checked here?"

"Sure." Daniel went to the desk and took the long wand a girl handed him, trailing ribbons and glowing with custom LEDs. "This is pretty." He held it against a dowel rod he took from the wall, and the ends matched perfectly. "Four feet, on the nose. Someone did her homework."

The costumed girl, wearing small translucent wings and radiant in sparkling makeup, smiled. "I had to grind the staff down so I could fit the finial under the limit. Can you tag it here—" she pointed to a handhold between two clusters of flowers and LEDs — "so I can cover it for photos?"

"Sure thing." Daniel fitted a zip tie around the staff where she had indicated and clipped the end. "Have a good con. Next?"

The armored teen passed a gun through, and Daniel checked it. "No moving parts, no functional barrel, orange tip. You're good to go." He attached another zip tie and passed the prop back to the teen.

Jacob selected a black and red shirt which read *Con Job Con Aid*. "When do you need me?"

Daniel turned to a dry erase board marked into a schedule. "Let me see…."

Another man came into the room and tossed two fake guns into another plastic bin. "No orange tips. Seriously, people, it's not hard. Orange tips." He looked at Daniel. "Is there a chance I can go off shift now? I think I got some bad tacos and trust me, it's better for everyone if I can just stay in my room for a while."

Daniel looked at Jacob. "How about now?"

Jacob pulled the shirt over his head, hooked the radio the other passed him to his waistband, and went to the table to add one of the Con Aid badges to his own. Daniel glanced down as he worked the badge holder snaps. "Put your full name right on your badge? That's bold."

Jacob shook his head. "Data entry mistake. Apparently

reg is hand-entering everything instead of using an automated system."

Vince gave a sad little half-smile. "Yeah, and they hate me for it."

"Hate you?" Jacob was pretty sure the registration department head had been a female name.

"I'm the con chair."

Jacob didn't know how to respond. "Uh, sorry."

Vince shrugged a single shoulder. "I know it's a pain, and it figures there would be mistakes. Rita wants to use an online ticketing service like we've done before, but those things cost a bundle, and frankly the con can't afford it."

Jacob swept his hand to indicate the hotel and convention center around them. "Not that I know anything about it, but this is a pretty good-sized con, and it's not a start-up. From the little I know, you should be on your feet pretty soon, if not already."

"We were," Vince said. "And then stuff happened."

The radio crackled, and Jacob felt for the volume knob as Daniel pulled an earpiece into place. "Go ahead."

Jacob couldn't hear the call, but he saw Daniel go still. He got the volume up again in time to hear, "…last stall."

Daniel didn't hesitate. "Empty and block the room. Stay in the doorway until I'm there. Don't touch anything. I'm on my way." He turned to Vince, who had sat up at the change in Daniel's tone. "Call 911 and ask for an ambulance; we've got a girl down in the east corridor restroom. You can meet us there. Jacob? Come with me."

Jacob felt a little thrill — Daniel was taking him to the scene! — along with a darker guilt for being excited while someone was hurt.

No, not hurt; Daniel had told whoever was at the other end of the radio to clear the room and not touch anything, and if the girl had been sick or injured he would have said to help her. They'd have to call an ambulance regardless. The "don't touch anything" was the clincher. They were going to a body.

Nothing really seemed to be wrong as they moved down the east corridor. It was a lower-traffic area, removed from the main hub of the convention. People moved through the hall, laughing and calling to friends or to costumes they recognized. The men's room was open, and a few guys in jeans and black t-shirts exited, but a chair blocked the women's door, and a college-aged man in a Con Aid shirt sat in it. Beside him stood a woman, slightly older, in a Sailor Moon costume.

As they neared, two girls approached the door, and the Con Aid staffed extended an arm to block them. "Sorry, restroom's closed. You'll have to go to the lobby."

"I just want to touch up," said one girl. "I think I smeared my eye."

"You want the lobby, trust me," said the Sailor Moon cosplayer. "It's a nasty backup. I'm only waiting because I left my phone in the back and I want the plumber to cross the puddle for it, not me."

The girls' faces screwed up in revulsion. "Ugh. Okay, thanks for the warning."

Daniel and Jacob stepped in as the girls left. "What do we have?" asked Daniel.

The Con Aid staffer looked at the Sailor Moon. "She found her."

"Woman in the last stall," the cosplayer said. "I was in the next stall, noticed the legs next to me weren't right. She was on the floor, mostly, kind of against the wall. I called to ask if she were all right, and when she didn't answer, I crawled under the door."

Daniel nodded. "And she's dead?"

"I can't declare that. But no respiration, no pulse, and she's cooling."

Daniel raised an eyebrow. "You an EMT?"

"Not so much, just Ski Patrol. I have basics, and I know enough to know I can't legally pronounce anything." She gave a tight, nervous smile. "So I stuck my head out here, and he was right close—" she indicated the Con Aid man — "and I figured I'd better stay long enough to answer any questions. Not that I know much, just, you know, I found her."

"You did right," Daniel said. He looked at the Con Aid man. "She can stay with you, and no one goes in except me. An ambulance is en route, and you can point them in. But unless I give someone the okay or they're wearing law enforcement badges, no one else."

He nodded, a little pale. Daniel glanced at Jacob. "Coming?"

"Wait." The Sailor Moon cosplayer licked her lips, but her voice was steady. "I think maybe no one else should go in except the police, right?"

"Good thought. And I am police." Daniel pulled a badge on a lanyard from the collar of his Imperial uniform. "Come on, Jacob."

The lack of urinals startled Jacob more than it should have. There were five stalls and three sinks, and the last stall door was closed. Jacob bent and saw a sprawl of legs in nude hose and sensible blue heels.

Daniel inserted the stiff edge of his Con Aid badge into

the outward side of the stall lock and turned it. The door swung open, and they looked down at the dead woman. She was fully dressed. She'd probably been facing the rear of the stall, perhaps leaning over the toilet, before she had fallen forward and slid between the stool and the restroom wall. One arm was beneath her, the other caught on the toilet seat, and her head was turned upward at an awkward angle.

The distortion of her distressed expression and bloated face was disturbing enough to rock Jacob, but they didn't keep him from recognizing her. It was the Dead-Laura cosplayer, looking more dead than ever.

Chapter Four

"She had a badge," said the uniformed officer. "Surely there's a way to find out who she is."

Vince Corleone shook his head. "Some cons number badges, we don't have any reason to. If she didn't have a custom name on the badge, there's no way to track it in the system." He shrugged, pushing his fingers through his hair. "They're tickets, not identification."

"She went by CosBright," Jacob offered. "And I might be able to get her phone number."

The officer turned. "You know her?"

Jacob shook his head. "Not exactly."

"This is Jacob Foster," Daniel said. "He's done some ride-alongs with me, plans to enter Academy this fall."

The other officer nodded, his face relaxing into friendliness. "Right on."

"Thanks," Jacob said. "I've been studying criminal justice, got one semester left. But I really want to get into the Academy."

"Keep your nose clean." The officer winked. "So, you sort of know the deceased?"

"Met her a few hours ago. Literally just bumped into her, but she talked to a friend of mine and they exchanged numbers."

"Would your friend have the name?"

"No, just CosBright." Under the officer's gaze, Jacob continued, "A lot of people do that in the con community, go by aliases or screen names. It's pretty common."

"Hm." The officer frowned.

"Not a criminal thing — it's left over from when geeky pursuits were really looked down on. People didn't want their bosses to know they were at a con over the weekend. But Sam's got her number, anyway, and you could do a lookup off that. And if she pre-registered CosBright as a badge name, it should be connected to her credit card or Paypal account."

"Spell it?"

Jacob hesitated. "I never saw it in print, just heard her say it. But I'd guess C-O-S-B-R-I-G-H-T, or maybe with a Z, or something like that."

The officer nodded and looked at Vince. "Can you have someone look that up?"

"Sure. But we don't have to say anything yet, do we?" Vince swallowed. "Not until we know more. This is a lot of people to panic."

The officer nodded. "Just have someone look up the name, if it's there. But there's no reason to panic; we don't have any evidence of foul play at this time. And you, get that number from your friend, but without making any waves."

Jacob moved away and dialed Sam's number, but the call was promptly sent to voice mail. A moment later a text arrived. *In a panel. What's up?*

Can you send me American Gods Laura's number?
Sure. What's up?
Later.
Right-o. When things got serious, Samantha didn't waste time with stupid questions. A moment later, his phone buzzed with the arriving number.

He glanced at Daniel and then started another text. Vince Corleone would probably flip out if he knew Jacob was telling anyone, but better for his aunt to hear it from Jacob than the news when it inevitably broke, and at least Jacob could be certain that she would keep it quiet. Lydia was professionally quiet about sensitive news.

A death at con, but not any of us or friends. Not public yet, just wanted you to know in case media goes nuts.

He pocketed the phone and went back. "I've got the number, if you've got a notepad or something."

"Good." Another officer had arrived, and she gestured to a chair. "Sit down, please, and copy it for me. Then I'd like you to tell me everything you noticed about the scene where you found her."

Jacob tensed. As a con attendee? Or as a Police Academy hopeful? No, they wouldn't want inferences. Just the facts, ma'am. "The stall door was closed; Daniel popped the lock with his badge. The dead woman was lying mostly between the toilet and the wall, kind of sprawled like she'd passed out or fallen. She was dressed, so she didn't fall off the toilet, but she had been vomiting or something. And she smelled kind of garlicky. I don't know if that's relevant at all, probably just what she was throwing back up."

The officer nodded. "Go on."

"We were pretty sure she'd be dead, from what the Sailor Moon said and how she looked, but Daniel checked her anyway." Jacob shrugged. "And then we came out to wait for the ambulance and officers."

The officer nodded. "About as Daniel said. I hear you're looking to enter the Academy?"

"I'm doing interviews next month."

"Good to hear. Good luck." She rose and went to speak with the others.

His phone buzzed, and Jacob read the incoming text. *Media always nuts, so thanks for heads-up. How'd you hear?*

Was there when security found her.

Need backup?

I'm okay, thanks.

Getting some detective practice in?

Very funny. It wasn't even a murder, in all probability, just an unfortunate death.

Chapter Five

Jacob swiped his key card and pushed back the hotel room door. "Tell me we have food."

A dozen or more people mumbled cheerful greetings through full mouths or waved as they chewed. Jacob slid into a gap against the wall and stretched for the pizza box Sam pushed toward him.

"You got stuck working late," Andrew of Fish Face Costumes commented. "They're really short on security?"

"A little short, but not bad now that they've picked up some extras." There was a slice of pepperoni left in the box.

"Sam thought you'd be back sooner. Anything wrong?"

Jacob stopped chewing and made steady eye contact. "I could tell you," he intoned, "but then I'd have to kill you."

Andrew laughed and went back to his pizza.

"You don't happen to know if Dead-Laura is going to make it, do you?" Sam asked. She hadn't mentioned his request, which was good, but she was letting him know that *she* knew that *he* knew something about her tardiness. "She was so excited about talking construction techniques, and I've texted her twice."

Jacob shook his head. "I don't think she'll be able tonight, sorry."

Sam glanced at Brittany, who shrugged. "We'll be here all weekend, if she gets a chance. And we're doing a couple of how-to panels tomorrow, so she can drop in there."

"I'll tell her," Sam said.

Jacob was rooting through the pile of discarded pizza boxes for another piece when Sam settled beside him. She opened her mouth, hesitated, and then spoke under her breath. "I hate to be the bearer of weird news, but...."

"What?"

"There was another episode playing. *Cougars and Cold Ones*, I mean. It was running when we arrived at the panel room."

Jacob exhaled and looked down at the cold slice of extra cheese.

"We shut it down. Had to, so the panel could start. But, you know, it's out there."

"It always is," he said. "Thanks."

The dinner crowd was fading, slipping away to get drinks at the bar or finish costumes or play Werewolf in the lobby. Sam stacked empty pizza boxes and handed them to Zach to put in the hallway. "This is the girls' bed," she said, pointing. "You guys have the window bed."

Jacob was the only one of the four who hadn't brought costumes, and he saw his backpack and duffel tucked between the bed and the wall to save space. "Got it."

Sam turned to face him. "So what really happened, or can you tell us? And why'd you need Dead-Laura's phone number? Did she get in trouble?"

Jacob bobbed his head from side to side, considering. "You could say that."

"Oh, no. What'd she do? She seemed nice."

Jacob exhaled. "She died." He gestured as the other

three looked sharply at him. "Keep it on the down-low. Word will get out, of course, but we don't want scary rumors running around."

"What happened?" asked Jessica. "Was she — attacked?"

"No, it didn't look anything like that," he said. "It was more like something internal, like she was sick or something. Maybe a food allergy, even."

"Whoa." Zach shook his head. "I guess some are that serious, right? Like peanuts or something?"

"I don't think it was peanuts," Jacob said. "I'm guessing she had Italian. Not to be rude, but she kinda smelled of garlic."

"That's a clue!" Jessica slapped her hands on her thighs. "Garlic scent — that's some sort of poison!"

"You read too many mysteries," Jacob said.

"Besides," Zach put in, "I think strychnine smells like almonds."

"That's cyanide," corrected Jessica, "and it smells like bitter almond, which is a different species than sweet almond. And no, the garlic scent is a clue. I can't remember what, but that's a poison."

Jacob turned his hands up in a helpless gesture. "Seriously, you can't just run with these things. Murder? Because she smells like garlic? It's not really that neat and tidy and contrived in real life. You know how hard it is to get a conviction now that juries expect everything to look like *CSI*?"

Jessica raised an eyebrow. "I just said she could have died of eating something poisonous. You're the one who brought up murder."

Someone knocked at the door, and he got up to answer it and avoid Jessica's eyes. Probably one of the pizza guests had forgotten something.

A girl with pink and purple hair — her own, not a wig — stood outside. A duffel bag hung over her shoulder. "Jacob! I saw you come in a while ago. I don't suppose there's a chance your floor is open, is there?"

"Um, hi, Amber. Do you not have a room?"

"Well, about that." She pushed purple-streaked hair back from her face. "I was supposed to be with Erika and people, because Tim dropped out because he had an exam he couldn't miss. So I took his spot. But then Tim talked his prof into letting him do the exam early, so he came anyway, only they forgot to tell me that he was back in, and they said because he was a part of the room first that he got first dibs, even though no one had told me and I'd picked up his spot."

"Can't you just sleep on the floor in there then?" asked Zach.

Jacob started shaking his head before Amber could answer; he knew how Erika and her friends afforded cons. "No room, right?"

"There's already twelve people, and it's got a shower, not a bathtub."

"Fine," Sam said, waving her in. "You can probably fit at the foot of the guys' bed. Safer than that fire hazard, anyway."

"The scent of garlic," announced Jessica, reading from her phone, "is a potential indicator for arsenic."

Jacob turned and gave her an incredulous look. "No one's killed anyone with arsenic since Agatha Christie retired."

"What about arsenic?" asked Amber, unrolling her sleeping bag.

"Nothing," Jacob said. "We're talking about pizza and Italian food."

"Ooh, is there any pizza left?"

Jacob sighed and pointed. "Over there."

Chapter Six

"We have got to do something about those green alien things," said Rita the registration DH as she came into the Ops office. "Some of 'em are smearing body makeup all over everything. Hotel's gonna eat us alive."

"I think they're grey," said Daniel. "Like aliens."

"Grey-green. Are aliens grey? Do we know that?"

"Greys are. Or the Silence. But these are from some web series."

"They're Moles," Jacob offered. "Yes, from a web series, crazy fan base. I don't follow it enough to understand it all, but they're all those alien Moles with little antennae and grey-green skin. There's a zillion of them — everything from high school students to space pirates to ancient Greeks. All Moles."

"Whatever," said Rita. "Point is, I just threw a kid off the lobby couch because he was leaving body paint on it. Vince is going to flip his skull when the hotel hits him with the cleaning bill." She shook her head. "I don't know why cosplayers have to be so irresponsible."

"Two of my roommates are doing body makeup this weekend," Jacob said defensively, "and they seal it all properly. They say it's mostly the young kids who are cheap and don't know what they're doing who make a mess."

"The young kids, whose parents drop them off like we're a freaking babysitting service," grumbled Rita. "You know how many twelve-year-olds are running around here on their own? What's wrong with people these days?"

Zach was some version of Hellboy for the day, and he'd spent the morning painting himself red. Jessica had started as one of the grey-green Moles — there were dozens or hundreds of characters, as Jacob had said, and he couldn't keep them straight — in a fluffy ballgown she'd made of chiffon and sparkles. She would change later, though; Jessica often did three or four costumes throughout a long convention day, for various photoshoots or to meet different friends.

Samantha was dressed today as a 1930s aviatrix, with boots and scarf and goggles, from some retro comic. She was carrying Jacob's copy of *How to Die in Five Easy Steps*, so that he wouldn't have to return for it when it was time to escort Greg Hammer to his autograph session. He'd reminded her again and again of how to fit it into her bag, of the importance of keeping it in mint condition, until she'd rolled her eyes and pushed him out into the hotel hallway.

Live music started in the lobby, a melodic ballad, and Rita raised her head. "That's got to be the Spork Minstrels," she said. They were a band specializing in video game music. "I like them. They add a bit of class, wherever they go."

Two men leaned into the half-open door, and one rapped at the door frame. "Excuse me? Is this headquarters, or whatever it's called?"

"Con Ops," said Rita. "What can I do for you?"

"Reporters," breathed Daniel, just loud enough for Jacob to hear.

"I'm Andy Timmerman, from the *Times*, and this is John Dresler, with the *Herald*. Is there someone we could talk to about what happened here last night?"

Jacob looked at Daniel, who nodded once. "You can smell 'em," he whispered.

Rita opened her mouth, closed it, and looked at Daniel

with mute appeal. He sighed. "What do you want to know, gentlemen?"

"A woman was found dead last night. Can you speak to her condition? Was it homicide or accidental?"

Daniel frowned. "Cause of death yet to be determined, no immediate indication of foul play. But you didn't have to come here to get that."

The reporters' ears practically pricked like interested dogs' as they came into the room. "Were you here at the time?" One raised a camera phone and snapped a shot of Daniel.

Daniel gave him a small glare which was only enhanced by his Imperial uniform. "You're here for some color to the story?"

"Well, you know, the convention is kind of… a colorful thing." The Times reporter had the grace to look a bit embarrassed, but only a bit.

"I was here," Daniel said. "Word came of an incident in the restroom, I responded."

They brightened. "And your name?"

"Sergeant Daniel Ratherman."

There was a moment of hesitation. "Sergeant?"

Daniel reached into his uniform jacket and withdrew the badge hanging on a lanyard about his neck.

The Herald cleared his throat and put on a look of suspicious annoyance. "You said there was no evidence of foul play, but then what's an undercover officer doing here?"

"Not undercover, just enjoying the con on his off-duty hours," Daniel said, "and volunteering to keep it running smoothly, like good con attendees do. Is there anything else I can help you gentlemen with?"

The door swung back and a stocky man in a tight green polo shirt pushed inside. "Is this Ops?"

"It is," said Rita. "What do you need?"

"Where is my freakin' coffee?"

Rita blinked. "Excuse me?"

"I need another guy, and some coffee. I'm out."

Rita raised an eyebrow. "Who are you?"

"Um," Jacob started, "this is Ryan Brazil."

"Ah," Rita said, her expression flat. "Sorry, I don't do anything with Guests. But what'd you need?"

"That guy who was supposed to be helping me, I sent him for coffee, and he just disappeared. What kind of aide is that? So I came here to get another."

"Another guest staffer, or another coffee?" Rita's expression hadn't grown more welcoming.

The Herald snapped a photo. "You're a guest here? Mind if we ask you a few questions?"

Ryan Brazil turned a caffeine-deprived stare on him. "Eh?"

The Herald produced a business card. "I'm —"

"Media," supplied Ryan, his stare dissolving into a smile. "Of course. Yes, I'm delighted to speak with you, and I'm sure there's an interview coordinator, yes?" He looked at Rita.

She was looking at a laptop screen. "I'm still not with Guests. You'll have to talk with Henry."

Ryan looked irritated but masked it as he turned back to the Herald. "Of course, I suppose we could take a few minutes now, rather than inconvenience you gentlemen later. What about the green room?"

The Times got the courage to ask first. "Er, what brings you here to the convention?"

Ryan's pasted smile wavered. "I'm Ryan Brazil. I'm a voice actor. I'm here as a media guest."

The Herald nodded once. "I'd be happy to take your media kit." He smiled, and Jacob realized he was trying to be kind.

Ryan didn't think so. "Just the kit? A headshot and a standard bio? It doesn't have anything about the upcoming *Mega-Nega-Racetrap* reboot."

The Times wasn't so kind. "What's that?"

"Only the most anticipated game franchise update since Lara Croft got de-pixelated boobs. I voice Nega Carson, the—"

"Actually, maybe you can help us," interrupted the Herald with only a slight air of desperation. "I don't suppose you were here last night when the body was found?"

Now Ryan blinked. "What?"

"Guys." Rita rose and closed the door, though the pass-through was still open to the streaming hallway. "We're trying not to panic people. What happened was tragic, but it's not worth scaring a whole convention."

"Wait, a real body?" said Ryan. "Like, a dead one?"

Daniel sighed. "A young woman was found dead in a restroom yesterday. Looked like she'd been ill. We haven't heard back on the autopsy yet, but as there was no reason to suspect homicide, we're keeping it on the down-low for the moment. Not a cover-up, but just trying not to shout it down the halls, either."

Ryan rubbed a finger across his eye. "I hadn't heard. Of course, I haven't heard much of anything this morning, since I'm still trying to wake up and my stupid coffee hasn't ever appeared."

"You can get some in the staff suite," Rita sighed. "Two doors down, conference room B."

Ryan's mouth twisted. "Somehow I doubt the staff suite stocks Starbucks Limited Auromar," he said. "I make a living off my throat, you know. I have to be careful what I put into it."

"You should think a bit about what comes out," Rita said, and before Ryan could respond she continued, "News guys, are you going to be here for a while, or do you have what you need?"

The Times and the Herald exchanged glances. "We really ought to get some photos, at least. Maybe cover the con a bit until we hear back on, you know, the victim."

"Fine. Then you'll need badges." She pulled a couple of blank media badges from a box and grabbed a marker.

"Not necessarily a victim," Daniel added.

"I guess we can do a local color angle," said the Herald. "Show off the con a bit, if there's nothing to the death."

"Could have been drugs," suggested the Times in a low voice. "You know, it's a whole hotel full of grown people playing games and dress-up. Not to generalize, but lots of losers here."

"Excuse me," rumbled Daniel. "The man in the Imperial uniform can hear you."

Ryan looked around the room pointedly for a moment, but when no one seemed to notice, he sighed audibly and said, "I guess I'll see what the staff suite has, then," and opened the door again.

As he exited, a woman came in, wearing a dark green pantsuit and her hair in an incongruous ponytail. "Is Vince Corleone in here?"

It was the VP from MEGAN!ME, and she didn't look any happier than the last time Jacob had seen her. He suspected that Vince wouldn't be any happier this time, either. "He's out for now," he offered, "but I can give him a message for you."

She looked at him as if she'd just been surprised by a talking doorknob. "I don't want to be put off by some unpaid volunteer," she said, dripping disdain. "I want to talk to Corleone. People are talking about a death at the convention, and I don't want MEGAN!ME associated with—"

A tall, thin man sporting a goatee and a *Season of the Dove* t-shirt came in. "Hey, has anyone—" He stopped, startled as he nearly bumped into the power-suited woman.

She turned on him. "I didn't realize you were here, Christopher. Thought you'd still be in a basement somewhere below your mother's kitchen."

"Um." He blinked and then seemed to recover, and a corner of his mouth turned down. "That doesn't surprise me much, Valerie. But if you'd bothered to check the program, you might have noticed that I'm a guest."

"Sorry you'll have to disappoint your fans," she answered. She turned back to Jacob. "Radio Vince and find out what he's doing about this bad publicity."

"It's not really bad publicity," Rita said. "No one's freaking out. A few people are talking, but it's more rumor than panic. Even the press isn't wigging out over it." She gave pointed looks to the Herald and the Times.

Valerie turned on them. "Are you media?"

The Herald cleared his throat. "I'm—"

"Never mind, I need Vince. Radio him and tell him I want to talk with him."

"What are we talking about?" asked the newcomer she'd called Christopher. "What bad publicity?"

Rita sighed. "A young woman died last night at the con. Probably a medical thing, not any kind of assault, but sad all the same."

Christopher's mouth dropped slightly open. "Oh, no."

"Which is why I need to talk to Vince," snapped

Valerie. "Somebody get him."

"I'll get right on that," Jacob volunteered. "Where should I have him meet you? It's getting pretty crowded in here."

She considered. "The hotel bar will be fine; it shouldn't be busy this time of morning."

"Got it. I'll tell him."

She pushed past the goateed Christopher and shoved into the hallway, already full of attendees. Christopher pushed the door shut behind her.

Daniel looked at Jacob. "Where should he meet her? Brilliant."

"It seemed logical," Jacob said. "And, well…. If he doesn't get the message, maybe she shouldn't have left it with some unpaid volunteer."

Daniel laughed. He pushed a button on the radio attached to his belt and spoke into the earpiece. "Chair, this is Con Aid. We have a Code SEP in the bar, repeat Code SEP in the bar."

Jacob fumbled his earpiece into place in time to hear, "Got it, thank you."

He looked at Daniel. "SEP?"

Daniel smiled. "Know your Douglas Adams? That's *Somebody Else's Problem.* Something to ignore, and in this case to avoid."

"Um," said Christopher. "With the, you know, are we still running full schedule and everything?"

"Paul's the programming DH," Rita said, "and he's grabbing breakfast in the staff suite, but I haven't heard anything about any changes. When's your stuff?"

"Eleven, in Main, for the game show, and then at three and five after that."

"As far as I know, everything should be fine, but if you want to wait a few minutes, Paul will be back and we can confirm. And hey, I was really sorry to hear about your show. That was rough."

"Thanks. It was pretty frustrating."

Jacob looked at him again. "Wait — you're Christopher Adams! I didn't recognize you."

He laughed, a little bitterly. "Yeah, I'll put it on for the game show, but the costume hurts a little right now." He looked back at Rita. "I'll just walk over and catch Paul at the staff suite. Thanks."

The Times looked after him, as if trying to decide whether he should be interested. "Who was that?"

"Christopher Adams. He's a BNF."

The Times looked blank.

"Big Name Fan. Famous for being a famous fan, I guess."

"Like celebutantes," contributed Rita, "but with more geek cred."

"He's usually in this crazy costume, the Terra Vista Ranger. Hilarious *sentai* thing. He pretty much had a career of being a fan, had a really popular web site and was even getting his own web series. But it got pulled when MEGAN!ME bought out FunFilms, which was his primary sponsor."

The Times, who had been looking more intrigued, seemed to lose interest again. "Oh. Could have been a good human interest story there. Too bad."

"Is this where we get props and weapons checked?" called a cosplayer at the window.

Jacob got up and checked the props, confirming that the fake firearms had orange tips and no moving parts and that the over-sized *shuriken* was less than four feet long, and he tagged them as approved. "Enjoy the con."

A girl in a Japanese schoolgirl *fuku* was next, but before she could speak Ryan Brazil pushed forward. "Oh, hello," he said to her. "What a lovely costume. You did a fabulous job on that."

She smiled and blushed. "Thank you."

"Really, it's very nice. Did you know I was in that show? I did the voice for Sato Kaname. Can I get a picture of you, when you're done here?"

"Sure." She grinned, a little embarrassed but pleased.

"You need your *katana* checked?" Jacob held out his hand for the mock weapon.

The Herald was standing beside him. "You measure everything?"

"Four feet or less, to keep hallway traffic safe and manageable. And we check all blades and firearms, to be sure they're fake."

"Is that a problem?"

"Not really. Mostly a precaution." He tagged the *katana* and returned it to the schoolgirl. "There was a case once, I think, of some sick jerk bringing a paintball gun to use on cosplayers, but that wasn't here. And it got shut down in a hurry."

"And, what's a cosplayer?"

Jacob gestured. "These guys, people in costume. Cosplay is short for costumed playacting."

"Like, make-believe for grownups?"

"My friend Sam calls it performance art. It's about craftsmanship and character."

"He does this kind of thing?"

"She does a lot of it, yeah. She's good, she's won some awards — but that's not why people do it. Like she says, it's more of an art for most people." He nodded toward the media badge clipped to the reporter's shirt. "You should go to the masquerade tonight. That's where all the best stuff will be."

"I know cosplay!" The Times sounded pleased with himself. "I've never actually seen it before, but I watched this show on TV about cosplayers—"

"No," several of them said together.

The Times looked around at them, startled. "You — you don't like it?"

"It's safe to say that for the most part we didn't view it as a fair and accurate representation of our community," Daniel said in a crisp, professional tone.

The Herald was typing into his phone. "So we should check out the masquerade tonight, get a real feel for it." He looked at Jacob. "Anything else I should know?"

"About the con? Man, I can't cover it in a sentence or two. You want me to walk you around a bit later, if I've got time?"

"I'd appreciate that."

A man came in with a half-full coffee and an air of frustration. "What is wrong with people?" he demanded of no one in particular.

"Paul, did Christopher find you? Are we still on schedule with everything?"

"What? Oh, sure. As long as we can keep an eye on everything. Someone's swapping discs to be funny, and I don't have enough staff to babysit all the viewing rooms."

Jacob's stomach tightened. "What do you mean?"

"Two more viewing rooms this morning, running some old reality show instead of the scheduled episodes. And a couple of panel rooms, first thing this morning, and people walked in to find it playing. I mean, I guess I should be glad it's not porn or something, but it's annoying."

Jacob knew, but he asked anyway. "What show?"

"Something older, Cougars and something. Does it matter?"

He shrugged over his stomach twisting. "Guess not."

But it did.

Chapter Seven

"Her name was Tasha Kurlansky," Daniel said. "They found her key card in her bra when they took her to the morgue, and the hotel was able to look up her room info. She was sharing with someone who says they met on the forums and had roomed a couple of times, but they didn't know each other well." He shook his head. "Which is admittedly a little weird, outside of a hostel, but on the other hand, roommate murders don't tend to be bloodless and in a public restroom, so it's pretty unlikely that anything came of that."

"Was it murder, then?" Jacob asked.

"Oh, no, not necessarily. Autopsy's going on now, most likely, and we'll hear if they learn anything."

"It feels so wrong to say I hope it was a food allergy or something," Rita said, "but you know what I mean."

"Yeah," Daniel said, "I do."

"Hey, Jacob," called Sam from the pass-through. "Can you tag my glaive for me?"

"What the heck is a glaive?" Daniel stood to see the prop.

"It's what the toughest knights wield in the toughest battles, of course." Sam held it up and gave it a little twirl in her hand. "Seven feet of pure evil-smashing kick-assery," she said, "and then — poof! — it breaks down into two conveniently hallway-approved economy-sized components." She twisted the weapon's long pole and it came apart. "I'll be carrying it tomorrow with my Spellknight."

"Nice," Daniel acknowledged. "Tag it, Jacob." He looked back at Sam and nodded toward Jacob. "You know this clown?"

She grinned. "He's my BFF. And I keep him put together. Here." She reached into the faux leather satchel at her waist. "I found your energy bar in the room where you forgot it."

"Thanks." Jacob took it.

"An energy bar? For serious?" Daniel assumed an overly-skeptical scowl. "Jacob, did you have breakfast?"

"Not after I walked out and forgot it."

"That's no good. Take advantage of the lull and go grab some real food. You're up to take care of Greg Hammer later, and it'll be embarrassing if your knees buckle and drop you in the middle of his autograph table." He grinned and added, "Seriously, three hot meals a day. Con rules for staff."

"I'm not staff, I'm a volunteer."

"Do not bother me with trifles," Daniel quoted. "After twenty years, at last my father's soul will be at peace." He nodded toward the door. "What's your name, girl?"

"I'm Samantha, but Sam is fine. Are you Daniel?"

"I see he's been talking about me behind my back."

"He told me about the ride-alongs and stuff."

"Yep. Sam, drag your BFF out for some real food. I've got a feeling it's going to be a long day, and a man needs some protein."

"Yessir." Sam saluted and came around to the door. "Let's go, Jacob."

They'd made it halfway across the lobby when Sam stopped dead. "Oh, wow," she breathed. "Look at that."

Jacob followed her eyes and saw a woman in breathtaking costume, where the hotel lobby opened onto the sunlit conservatory. "Oh, wow."

She wore something inspired by Chinese or Japanese history — Jacob wasn't knowledgeable enough to tell which — and probably at the level of imperial court finery even before it had been tricked up for stylization. Schooled by friendships with enthusiastic cosplayers, Jacob counted at least ten distinct layers of pastel color in her sleeves, and her outer layers spread wide about her in stunning pattern and color. The topmost layer was solid white, with white and silver embroidery over all the torso and down the sleeves. The sleek, dark wig was elaborately styled, high and twisted and smooth, and a riot of intricate jewelry and sashes ran over the entire thing, rather like a cage dress in semi-precious stones.

"That has got to be something from CLUTCH," Sam said. "I don't recognize it, but that amount of crazywork makes it a good bet. Probably something from one of the artbooks. Look at the sheen on it! Those under-layers have got to be silk, and I'll bet hand-dyed to get that kind of color." The cosplayer raised an arm to spread the sleeve for the crouching photographer, and Sam gripped Jacob's arm. "Oh — look at that lavender to pink gradient!"

"You need professional help," Jacob told her. "I wonder if there's a cosplay rehab clinic or something."

"Oh, come on. You can't tell me that isn't gorgeous."

He conceded. "No, I can't."

The photographer, a young black woman Jacob recognized, shifted slightly and waved an assistant to adjust the external flash he held. She had a real name, but Jacob could only recall that most people knew her as Laser, for her Laser Focus Photography. She shot several more photos, spoke to the cosplayer who moved her chin a half inch to the left, and took two more.

"I really want to talk to her, but not while she's in a

shoot," said Sam. "I'll try to catch her afterward. Because that's amazing."

"After food," Jacob said firmly. "I have to eat now, or I won't be back in time to escort Greg Hammer, and I'm not missing that."

"Right." She started forward, but she kept looking back over her shoulder as the cosplayer knelt and spread the outer layers.

"Come on," Jacob prompted. "Maybe she'll get lunch after she's done."

"Are you kidding? That thing's not going within a hundred yards of the food court. She's probably got a restraining order against ketchup."

The food court lines were already long, though the lunch wave wouldn't hit for another hour or two, and they chose a counter offering something called "breakfast gyros," mostly because its line seemed to be moving most quickly. "Any word yet on, you know, last night?" Sam asked.

"Nothing yet. But I don't know if there will be, either. I mean, it's not like they have to notify us if she died of a food allergy."

"That'd be sad." They shuffled forward in line. "But man, I hope that's all it is. Can you imagine if it were murder?"

"What do you mean?"

"This would be the worst place ever for a murder! For investigating, I mean." She put on a stern, deadpan voice. "Who were the last people seen with the victim? Eren Jaeger and a *Star Wars* stormtrooper? Quick, men, look for Eren Jeager and a stormtrooper! There are only twelve hundred or so here at the convention."

Jacob laughed. "We'll just have to hope that it's a more

standout costume then, like your CLUTCH piece."

They had picked up their breakfast gyros, which turned out to be just scrambled eggs and salsa in a pita, and were searching with increasing pessimism for an empty table when Jacob's phone rang. He balanced his food in one hand and pulled it from his pocket. "What's up, Daniel?"

"You aren't answering your radio."

"I'm on break, I don't have my ear in."

"Get back here. We got the autopsy results, and it's not good."

Chapter Eight

Daniel gestured Jacob into the staff suite and closed the door. Without a pass-through, this room was much more private, and Jacob guessed at the news. "So it wasn't a food allergy."

"Poisoned," Daniel confirmed.

Jacob shook his head. "But — why? She wasn't here with anyone.... Was it some date rape drug gone wrong?"

"No, and that's the weird thing," Daniel said. "She was poisoned with arsenic, and that hasn't been a murder tactic since it was a cliché. So it could be accidental, just because it's so weird and people do sometimes get accidental exposure. But it means we're now officially investigating a potential homicide."

Jacob felt the guilty little thrill again when Daniel said *we* and reminded himself that the word was meant generally. "So, what are you going to do, interview the whole con?" He remembered Sam's joke. "Oh, man, this is going to be impossible."

"So we're going to need every pair of eyes," Daniel said. "You can't do much on the record — any unusual participation or investigation would jeopardize a conviction if we did find a perp — but run it by me if you have any brilliant ideas. Because yeah, a victim without any real connections in a non-assault death at a convention like this, it's going to be rough."

Jacob nodded and tried to look appropriately serious.

He really was sorry for Dead-Laura's death — he had liked her, the little he'd known her — but the excitement of participating in the investigation, even a tiny unofficial bit, was undeniable.

"And not to minimize the significance of her death," Daniel continued, "but this could end Con Job. I don't know everything that's going on, but Vince has let on that the con's not doing well right now, and refunds or a drop in next year's attendance would pretty much be the death knell."

"It's not the con's fault," Jacob said, but he knew as he said it that it didn't matter. The public looked for something to blame, always, and rationality took a back seat.

Daniel's phone buzzed, and he drew it and read the screen. "Well, that's it, then," he said. "Update on the autopsy, and arsenic was in the stomach contents. Someone put it in her food. No way that's accidental."

Jacob looked at the remainder of his breakfast gyro. "Do we know what food?"

"Not for certain. She'd recently had an energy bar, a milkshake or something similar, and an order of fries, but it's not clear if any of them were the mechanism." He followed Jacob's eyes. "Surely someone isn't randomly poisoning the food court? Nah. There are thousands of people here, so statistically we should have already heard if someone was doing something like that." He sighed. "Finish your breakfast, and I'm going to go call everyone in. Vince wants to have a meeting about this, get us all on the same page." He went out, presumably to Con Ops.

Jacob sat for a moment and eyed his breakfast gyro. Only a couple of bites left; if it was going to poison him, he was probably already doomed. He gathered it into a sloppy handful and forced himself to swallow it.

Dead-Laura had eaten a series of snacks, it seemed, and it was impossible to guess where she'd bought them, or even if it had been at the food court or outside the hotel. There wasn't much around the convention center, but she could have even picked something up en route to the con.

Dead-Laura had been glad to be invited to dinner, and she hadn't mentioned bringing anyone else. And she'd made room-sharing arrangements online, with someone who said they weren't close. She'd been at the con alone, meeting people she knew only casually. So who at the con would have reason to kill her?

But if it were somehow a con attendee, rather than someone from Dead-Laura's personal life, then they needed to find a suspect fast. Because Sam was right, it would be hard to even track down the right people to question, and then tomorrow night the con would end and the attendees would scatter across several states, with only Registration's troubled hand-entered spreadsheet to identify them. And those who bought badges at the con itself, paying with cash, might have no record at all. And then Con Job would fail forever, and Dead-Laura's murderer would probably escape for good.

Jacob stared at the gyro's empty wrapping. This was going to be difficult.

He drew out his phone and typed a message to Lydia. *Death last night turns out to be a poisoning homicide. Really freaky. Going to be an interesting investigation, and I'll help where I can.*

This was exactly what he'd wanted to do. He'd wanted to go into Homicide for years, since he'd started thinking a real career was a possibility. He would have to put in his time and earn his way to Detective, of course, but this was his chance to shine going into the Academy. Daniel trusted him to help; he had to use his con knowledge.

His phone buzzed. *Coming. Don't panic, I'll be good.*

"What exactly are we supposed to do?" asked Vince, gesturing in frustration. "We announce there's a murder, people freak out. And not entirely without reason. We could tell them it was poison, so they should eat only from the food court or a reliable source — but she might have been poisoned at the food court, for all we know. So we don't know if that will protect people or expose them to some sicko employee who's poisoning random people for fun." He shook his head. "Or we could tell everyone to go home, which pretty much kills Con Job forever, not to mention makes a clean getaway for any sicko who's not a food court employee."

The assembled department heads shook heads, bit lips, and generally looked bleak.

"We need to know who she was with," Daniel said, "and where she went. We can open that up, ask people to step forward if they know anything. It's easy enough to spread the word; we can use the con mobile app or Twitter."

"Start with her screen name," Jacob said. "Ask for friends of Cosbright to come forward. That will at least narrow the field to something manageable, and we can always widen it if we need more."

Daniel nodded. "And a room where we can talk with people in private. Even one of the hotel rooms will —"

The staff suite door swung open. "I'm sorry," said a short, prematurely-balding man. "I did see the sign about a private staff meeting, but no one in Ops wanted to make the decision."

Vince sighed with frustration, but his voice remained

civil. "What do you need, Mickey?"

"I'm slated to lead a game of Murder tonight. I kind of suspect it would be in bad taste now, you know? But I wanted to check with you guys before my panel in a half-hour, so I know what to tell people there about an official schedule change."

Vince ran a hand through his hair. "Can you improv something? Stories from behind the scenes, trivia, question and answer?"

Mickey nodded. "I'll tell Ops, and they can post the schedule change."

Vince turned to Paul. "You can update the mobile app as soon as we're done here, right?"

"That's why we have it."

"Thanks, Mickey. We'll take care of it."

The man closed the door, and Rita pointed a pencil at it. "Who's that?"

"Mickey Groene, from *Star Chase*. Played Lieutenant Stafford. Does mostly voice work now." Vince looked at him. "You don't know the show?"

Rita shook her head. "Sorry."

"Well, you can't know everything at a con like this," Vince conceded. "Con Job is pretty broad, lots of fandoms, and that's one of the reasons people like us. Let's keep it that way, and find out what happened to this poor young woman, and with any luck at all it'll turn out to be nothing whatsoever to do with the con. But keep stuff calm. We've got to find out what happened without panicking anyone. We can't afford to lose this weekend."

They adjourned the meeting, and Jacob trailed the others back to Con Ops, testing announcement wordings in his head. *Would anyone who knew Cosbright please come forward? The police are seeking information regarding her movements yesterday.* Did that sound too scary? Would it put off potential witnesses?

Paul sat down at a laptop and began updating the schedule, replacing the Murder game with Mickey Groene's alternative programming.

Vince took a deep breath. "Okay, is anything else urgent at the moment? I mean, of course yes, but really, really urgent? Because I haven't eaten yet today, and I still haven't seen Valerie Kimberton, and I can only put her off for so long before she flips out and finds some legal way to yank their sponsorship and break us over her knobbly knee." He sighed again. "And I think I want a drink, I don't care if it is before noon." He turned and pointed. "Paul, you have the con."

"What?"

"What? It's a pun. You know how whenever the captain leaves the bridge he passes control to another officer with, You have the conn? Like when Captain Kirk…. Never mind. I'll be back as soon as I find some protein and a beer, in either order."

Sirens came distantly through the babble of hallway conversation, and Vince sighed. "I guess that's going to be how it is."

Daniel shook his head. "Shouldn't be any sirens, not for an investigation like this. That's emergency."

"Maybe they're just passing," Jacob suggested.

But the sirens grew louder, and then they seemed to plateau at moderately loud, and then they shut off abruptly rather than fading away again with distance.

Vince shoved his earpiece into position and spun the volume dial on his radio. "Does anyone know what's going on outside with the sirens? Are those for us?"

No one answered, and he called again. Finally someone

responded, "I don't know anything, but I see the ambulance team. Got to be something in the hotel. I'm following, will let you know what I learn."

"Where are you?"

"Mezzanine. Heading toward the central elevator well."

Vince jerked his head. "We're on our way."

As they hurried toward the elevators, the Con Aid member reported further. "EMTs won't answer questions, I'm not staff. Past the well, toward the bar, still following."

They took an escalator, skipping steps.

"At the hotel bar. It's not serving yet, but they're going in. They — there's somebody on the floor. Not moving. They're checking her, but they don't…. They don't look like they're in a big hurry."

Vince swore.

"I — I think it's that MEGAN!ME lady. I don't remember her name. But it looks like her."

Chapter Nine

Valerie Kimberton had been dead for nearly an hour, they thought, before the EMTs had arrived. It was hard to say for certain just yet, but the gamers who had found her while looking for empty tables for card games had called 911 immediately, and she had not responded to their shaking or well-meaning attempts to check for a pulse.

Vince was leaning over a table in the staff suite, surrounded by department heads again, ignoring the vegetable tray beside him as he rested his temples in his hands. "There was nothing wrong with her yesterday. It's another death, and that can't be an accident. It's going to be murder for her, too. That means some psychopath is randomly picking off con-goers."

"Why random?" prompted Daniel.

"Because if anyone wanted to murder that woman, I'd be first in line." Vince blinked. "Oh. Oh, no."

Jacob pressed his lips together. Daniel cleared his throat. "Just a friendly word of advice, Vince: you might not want to say things like that in front of other people."

Vince looked at Daniel, his eyes a bit wide. "But — I'm going to be a suspect, aren't I? I mean, everyone saw us arguing, right in the dealer hall. If they do any probing...."

The staff suite was very quiet, and the enthused laughter and calls from the hallway were loud through the door.

"Given the circumstances, they'll rush the autopsy,"

Daniel said to the room in general, "and unlike the first incident, we have a pretty good idea of where Valerie went and who she was talking to. So yes, everyone will be questioned — but don't panic, because questioning is a long way from detaining or charging, right?"

"Right," said Rita slowly. "I guess they have to talk to everyone. Just to be sure."

"Exactly. So don't panic, and be forthcoming. Don't try to hide things. We all know, for example, that she was making Vince's life difficult — but if you whitewash that, pretend there was nothing to that when there obviously was, it just makes things look suspicious. But, of course, you don't have to answer anything you don't want to."

Vince sighed. "What do we do about the convention?"

Paul shook his head. "I don't know that there's anything we *can* do. I mean, a moment of silence across the con, maybe? But it's not like we have any idea of what happened. And there's still a chance that they're not connected, or that Valerie wasn't even murdered." He sounded more hopeful than he looked.

Vince sat up. "Okay. We announce to the con that two people have died, but we make it clear that there's no established connection yet. We're going to get more Con Aid calls for certain as people worry, so I'm sorry, but you guys are probably going to have to extend shifts — and Daniel, I assume you're going to be putting on your other hat, but I'd appreciate any liaison work or guidance you can give as we go."

"Of course."

"Now, are those two reporters still around?"

"They went for lunch," Rita reported, "but they have media badges."

"I think we should have someone showing them around," Vince said. "Explaining the con, so they don't write us up as a bunch of maladjusted basement-dwellers, and keeping them from hyping some attendee into a sensational interview about panic at the con." He looked around the room. "I know we've all got full plates, but just, if you see them, check in on them, okay? Just show them around, bore them to death with lack of panic and criminal drama, and get rid of them."

"The one seemed pretty easy-going," Rita said. "And Daniel gave the other one the stink-eye. I think it'll probably be okay."

Vince continued, "And we need someone managing things in Ops, handling questions and keeping rumors down. Rita, you'll be in there anyway, and Reg should be slowing down soon; think you can handle that?"

She shrugged. "I'll try."

"Good enough. That's all we're doing at this point. Nobody plans for this."

Jacob raised a finger. "I was supposed to do escort for Greg Hammer and his autograph session...." *Please don't make me give that up. I know this is all crazy, but I want that.*

"When?" Vince glanced at the schedule on the mobile app and sighed. "Yeah, we need someone on that. Hammer's too big to leave on his own."

"Right."

"I'm going to post a new schedule," Daniel said, "of times for each of us to talk individually to the officers in the investigation. Let me know when you absolutely cannot make it, but we need everyone and it'll be easier if we have a plan. It'll be on the wall there as soon as I can make it happen."

Daniel's phone buzzed, and he checked the screen. His mouth thinned. "Autopsy's not done," he said, "but preliminary findings are arsenic in the stomach contents. Same poisoning as the other one. We're looking at a multiple homicide."

Chapter Ten

Jacob stopped in the Con Ops room to log himself out for Greg Hammer duty. A knocking sound caught his attention, and he turned, scanning for its origin. It was coming from the pass-through, where a woman was smiling and knocking on the wall. "Hello?" she called.

"Sorry," Jacob said, starting toward her. "Not used to polite knocking, not in this racket. People usually just yell if they want something."

She continued to smile, a little apologetically, and pushed a tablet toward him. He took it, confused, and bent his head to read the screen.

I am hearing impaired, so writing is easier for me in a noisy environment like a con. Sorry for the inconvenience!

"Oh, it's no inconvenience!" Jacob said, and then he felt himself blush. The woman laughed. "Sorry," Jacob said, wondering if he were compounding the problem.

She laughed again and scrolled. *I was coming to the con with a friend who was going to interpret at panels and events for me, but she closed her hand in a car door yesterday —*

"Ow!" said Jacob.

— and can't do it today. I know the con probably didn't plan for an interpreter on site, but is there a way you can put out the word for anyone here to interpret? I'm happy to compensate someone for the events I'm most interested in. Thanks for any help you can give.

Jacob gave her a smile and brought up the tablet's

keyboard. *We can certainly put out the word via the mobile app, and let me ask a friend who might be able to help out. He's either certified or testing soon, he'll probably be happy to help. And sorry again!*

She gave him a friendly smile.

Jacob took out his phone and texted Zach. *You available? Got an attendee here who lost her sign interpreter.*

When does she want someone?

Sounds like she's willing to negotiate.

Are you at Ops? I'll be right over.

"He's coming," said Jacob before catching himself, and then he smiled apologetically. He reached for the tablet, but she caught it and shook her head, laughing again.

Sometimes cons had interpreters for Main Programming and other big rooms that pulled thousands for the primary events, but it wasn't consistent. It was a shame her friend had been injured. Jacob wondered briefly if the friend were a professional interpreter and therefore was out of work until her hand healed.

Zach arrived in a surprisingly short time and signed a greeting. Jacob stifled a laugh at Hellboy signing with the petite attendee, but it seemed they were getting on well, and he had a guest to escort.

Greg Hammer was a tall man, lean with a bushy mustache and a buckskin jacket, which was completely at odds with his lime green running shoes. He held open the door of his hotel room and gave Jacob a friendly smile. "Are you my shadow for today?"

"For the next few hours, anyway. I'm Jacob." Jacob hesitated, debating, and then held out his hand. "I'm a huge fan of your work."

Greg's smile broke into a grin. "Hey, thank you, Jacob! That's great to hear. Thank you." He reached down and picked up a cardboard box. "Shall we?"

The elevator was empty when they boarded on the executive floor, but they picked up a few passengers as they descended. The first two didn't seem to pay any particular attention, and Jacob guessed they didn't know or didn't care who Greg was. The next pair of young women, however, recognized him. "Ohmigawd, Greg Hammer! We're so glad you're here. Except, I really wish you weren't here so you could be working on the next volume of *Madhouse*. Can I just say that you got me through grad school without completely losing my sanity?"

Greg laughed, shook hands, and opened the cardboard box to give them each a promotional postcard. "I can't say anything now, but there's going to be a *Madhouse* announcement next month. Keep your ears open."

"You bet!"

The first two passengers were watching now, aware they were in the presence of a celebrity but unwilling to show ignorance by asking about him. The girls got off, and on the second floor Jacob and Greg exited and started for the autograph area.

"So, I don't know what you've heard so far," Jacob began, feeling awkward, "but — there's no good way to say this — two people have died at the con. Poisoning in something they ate, but not food poisoning, if you follow. So police are investigating and you'll see them around, but we're not supposed to be shutting down or panicking or anything. If that makes sense." The Academy probably had whole classes on how to say this sort of thing, only Jacob hadn't taken them yet.

Greg hadn't heard. "Oh, no! Attendees?"

"One attendee, and one industry person. You probably didn't know Valerie Kimberton, with MEGAN!ME?"

"Yes, but only distantly. MEGAN!ME is actually making a bid to co-produce *How to Die* with a Japanese company as an anime. It's in negotiations, but that's less to do with me personally." Greg shook his head. "They have any ideas on what happened? Accident in the food court or something?"

"No one else seems to be getting sick," Jacob said. "This way, we can get in the back."

The autograph table was at the end of a line of stanchions and ropes which folded upon itself in a long zig-zag, already full of waiting fans. They clapped and cheered as Greg appeared from behind the ubiquitous convention center curtains. There were several chairs at the table, as sometimes several guests shared the table at once, but Greg Hammer had it all to himself.

He waved in a friendly manner, opened the box to sort promotional postcards and bookmarks across the table, and dropped a handful of markers in different colors and metallics on the table, ready to take on any surface he was asked to sign. Then he settled himself into the chair and beckoned the first attendee toward him. "Come on over! What do you have there?"

Jacob put himself at the end of the table, not quite between the head of the line and Greg Hammer, but he didn't expect to be anything more than an obligatory figure. Con Job's attendees were generally well-behaved and polite. Most geek cons were like that, actually. Grabbing at clothes and ripping off souvenirs was for rock concerts, not conventions.

Fans had brought mostly issues of graphic novels or compilation volumes to be signed, though some had t-shirts or figurines. One had brought a DVD with a poorly-colored cover, which made Greg howl with laughter. "Oh, where did you ever find this? Did you actually buy it? Are you the one?"

Jacob shifted to look at the table. He hadn't known about a DVD.

Greg held up the disc package and spoke to the fans around him. "This is a 1997 straight-to-video monstrosity of *Road Trip*, and there's a very good reason you've never heard of it. I thought it would destroy my career — only I was lucky enough that it failed so hard no one ever heard of it." He signed the cover with a flourish and handed it back to the grinning fan. "Keep it secret, keep it safe. And for Cthulu's sake, keep it out of reach of small children or the easily influenced."

Jacob drew out his phone and texted Sam. *I'm at the autograph table, don't see you. You coming?*

I'm about two-thirds of the way back, behind Naruto and River Song. Who are together, in fact. No, silly, I didn't forget you!

Jacob sent her a smiley face.

About forty-five minutes before the scheduled end of Greg Hammer's autograph session, Jacob went to the rear of the line and closed off the opening in the stanchions so no one else could join. They should wrap up on time.

Sam was indeed in line behind a Naruto (Shippuden version) and a Dr. River Song. She gave him a smile and wave as he passed.

When she reached the front of the line, drawing Jacob's copy of *How to Die in Five Easy Steps* from her messenger bag, Jacob stepped forward. "And, this one is actually mine," he said with a smile. "I'd be really honored if you signed it."

"Wow, a first edition." Greg turned it over. "And great condition. Can I sign the title page? The cover's still too gorgeous, I hate to screw it up with my messy scrawl."

He checked Jacob's badge — "With a c or a k?" — and then wrote out a short message and signed the page. Then he handed it back to Sam. "I'll let you hang on to that for him. Hey, is that a *Savage Air* costume?"

"Right on," she said. "Barnstorming Betty, the Junior Ace!"

"Highly under-appreciated series," he said. "Love it."

Sam and Jacob thanked him, and then Jacob stepped to the side with her as the next fan approached. "I'll leave this in the room," she said. "I have to hurry, 'cuz there's a gathering for *Savage Air* I just heard about, and I want to join. Laser is shooting it, so it'll be awesome."

"Let me know how it goes."

It was early afternoon when Jacob returned Greg to his room to pack, and he went back to Con Ops. As promised, there was a new schedule on the wall, showing staffers' names and interview times. Some already had check marks beside them. "Anyone seen the reporters?"

"They're out in the wild," Paul answered, tapping at the computer. "But I think Vince was being a little paranoid about that. We have media all the time, and aside from the occasional SOB, most of them write up human interest angles or even artsy stuff about the films and costumes. I wouldn't worry about it."

Jacob nodded. Paul was probably right.

"Do you think we'll get a lot of kickback if we push the *Magic: The Gathering* tournament back an hour? Gamers like late nights, right?"

Rita leaned over the pass-through. "Where's Vince?"

"I dunno. What's up?"

"Hotel staff is stripping the con suite. All the food, gone. They're taking everything."

Chapter Eleven

Paul radioed for Vince, who arrived at the con suite, surveyed the carnage of empty serving tables, and disappeared again in the direction of the hotel's hospitality offices. He wasn't gone long.

"Our liaison was looking for me," he said. "But they weren't going to wait until they talked to us."

"What's going on?" Rita asked.

"One of the hotel kitchen staff found a zipper bag of white powder stashed on the bottom of a catering cart. Management called police, thinking it was maybe drugs. Initial word is it's probably not cocaine, but it could be something bad — and since we've had two poisoning victims in less than twenty-four hours, they're pulling everything."

"Everything?"

"Staff suite, the hotel restaurants, the cash sandwich buffet, all of it. The food court is still open, because each of those franchises has its own kitchen, but they're being told to check over everything and there's a chance they'll be closed, too."

Paul gaped. "But we have thousands of people here. And a lot of these are kids without transportation or people who took shuttles in; they can't drive out to get food."

"The food court is still open for the time being. And there are the food trucks outside, though they were just to pick up overflow and were never intended to handle the whole con. Still, it's something, until we hear more."

"We can ask the hotel to waive in-and-out parking fees," Rita said, "so those with cars can get off-site. They should be reasonable about that, since it's their kitchen where the stuff was found."

"That's still going to leave a lot of people stuck if the food court goes down."

Vince nodded. "I'm working on it. Meanwhile, let's keep on keeping on. Jacob, what's your next move?"

Jacob glanced at the shift schedule on the wall. "Um, I'm going on lunch." He smiled grimly.

"Right." Vince grimaced. "You'd better hurry."

Jacob had to weave through an entire tribe of Water Benders to reach the *Star Trek* photo gathering at the far end of the conservatory. Below the glassy wall, a mob of red shirts held various frozen poses of clutching throats, pressing hands to imaginary chest wounds, or folding onto the ground in awkward positions as onlookers laughed and dozens of cameras and phone cameras snapped.

Jacob looked around until he found Jessica, dressed as an *Enterprise*-era Vulcan. "Hey, are you busy?"

She gestured to the red shirts. "Middle of a photo gathering, but I can talk until Vulcans are called. What's up?"

"You knew about arsenic having a garlic smell."

She nodded. "I read a lot of old cozy mysteries, even though some of them have a really skewed and outdated view on classism—"

"Yeah, but what I need to know is, how does one get arsenic poisoning?"

"In old cozy days? It was everywhere, used as a pesticide. Anybody could buy it. Nowadays it's harder to come by. Because, you know, it's toxic."

The red shirts released their poses and moved to join the onlookers. Someone called directions, and several Captain Kirks, Mr. Spocks, two Uhuras, three Mr. Sulus, and a Dr. McCoy assembled and stood at attention.

"Hang on," Jessica said, "lemme grab a shot of this." She aligned the crew in her phone's screen and snapped a couple of pics.

The conservatory featured lots of smaller gathering areas beneath one angled roof, incompletely separated by planters and couches in the ubiquitous sour colors of convention center furniture. The greenery did not adequately screen the next group photoshoot, featuring dozens of colorfully anthropomorphic ponies and interpretations.

"No idea on how someone would get it?" Jacob pressed. "Arsenic?"

"I presume you can get it somewhere, of course. Chemical supply companies, chemistry labs, really old warehouses full of illegal pesticides? Other than that, no, I've got nothing."

A photographer, squatting and looking into his bulky camera, shook his head. "We've got to change angles; it's like the *Enterprise* command is getting stalked by *My Little Ponies*. Everyone shift to your right."

The cosplayers obediently shifted to one side, laughing as they glanced back at the faux ponies.

Jacob shook his head. "Okay, thanks anyway."

He left Jessica with the *Star Trek* crowd and started for the food court. It was more than a little unnerving to enter the ring of fast food options — and was it his imagination, or did the court seem less over-crowded than usual? — but his stomach was growling and he had long hours yet ahead of him; he'd never make it without eating.

He looked around the food court and thought of Dead-Laura's fallen, twisted body and garlicky odor.

Vince had mentioned food trucks, and those were wholly separate from the hotel. And they wouldn't have been on site yet when Valerie ingested a fatal dose of arsenic this morning, so she couldn't have gotten it from any of them.

He consulted the mobile app and found the specified side street outside the convention space. He turned and headed for the doors.

A row of parked food trucks stretched outside the hotel, hawking everything from barbecue sandwiches to cupcakes to vegan stuffed potatoes. Jacob got in line at a pasta truck, perusing the blackboard menu. Someone had been having some fun tailoring the truck's offerings for the weekend crowd: *The Full-Melty Alchemist. The Trouble with Dribbles Minestrone. Second Breakfast Egg Sandwich. Witch Hunter Ramen. Arroz Khan Pollo. To Serve Manicotti. Spaghetti and Spaceballs. Dalek-table Chocolate Brownie.*

Behind him, a young man in full elven armor got in line. Jacob turned and gave him a nod. "Nice! First movie?"

"Helm's Deep, actually."

"Looks good."

"Looks stupid," said a man behind him. "What are you supposed to be, some sort of dress-up warrior? Why are you in a skirt?" He frowned. "Are these things feathers or leaves or what?" He plucked at the armor on the elf's shoulders.

"Please don't," said the elven archer, politely but shortly, as he stepped toward Jacob.

"What? I wasn't doing nothing." But he sneered as he shifted his weight forward.

There wasn't much room for Jacob to advance in the line, and he edged sideways to give the elf room to move. The man was facing them both, waiting in line but somehow more intent, and beside him stood a grinning friend. Both were wearing NFL jerseys, and both were a head taller than Jacob.

"So what is this freak show, anyway?" asked the one who hadn't spoken yet. "I thought if we came in the day before the game we'd beat the crowds."

"It's a convention," Jacob said. "For fans."

"Fans?" echoed the man with a sneer. "Fans tailgate. Fans cheer and support the team. Fans don't play dress-up."

"That's funny, coming from you," said a slender woman with a dark pixie cut from behind him. She had a yoga figure beneath her jeans and fitted green t-shirt, and her casual posture emphasized every curve. "Or are you both really pro football players?"

They turned to the new woman in line. "Are you with this con thing?"

"Hm? Oh, no. No badge, see? I'm here for lunch, same as you."

"Yeah." His eyes ran over her, resting on the emerald curves. "You need someone to walk you around, maybe keep the freaks back?" He jerked his head to indicate the lines of costumed attendees on either side of them. "Sometimes people can get a little — well, anyone who dresses like that. Kind of runs up a flag, you know."

"Oh, I do," she said. "But it's pretty easy to pick out the scary ones, if you keep your eyes open."

"Yeah?"

"Oh, yeah, you just look at what they dress as. For example—" she pointed at the elf — "that's one of Haldir's archers. He came to defend a bunch of trapped innocents and fight to certain death, just because it was the right thing to do for a former ally." She pointed further ahead in line, where others were starting to notice the conversation. "That guy in the plaid shirt and vest, next to the redhead? He waited two thousand years for her to wake up and remember him, protecting her all that time." She turned to the next line, where Tony Stark was paying for a Ham Solo sandwich. "That guy carried a nuke through a rift, thinking it was a one-way trip, to save his friends. In the cine-verse, anyway."

"What?"

"See the group over there? The tall one, he gave up his elite medical career and cushy privileged lifestyle to rescue his abused sister and hide her on the ragged frontier of space."

"What are you talking about?"

She turned back to face them. "And you're dressed like a man charged with real-life murder. And you, you're wearing the number of a man convicted of felony assault against a police officer." She crossed her arms. "So yeah, some people can really send a message."

The men squinted at her. "What are you saying?"

"Me? I'm not saying anything in particular, just pointing out who people are dressing up like."

"Why can't I wear this? I'm a fan!"

"Hey, I think people can wear just about anything they want. And this guy chose to dress as a selfless hero." She met the elf's eyes and smiled.

"Bitch," said one of the men.

Her eyes didn't flicker. "I was right, wasn't I? Helm's Deep?"

The elf hadn't expected her to speak to him. "Uh, yeah. Yeah, you were right."

"I thought the color was right."

"Are you a costumer?"

"No, but I do have some figures. I'm sort of an uncommitted collector."

"Forget this," snapped one of the jersey men. "This line's too long anyway."

"Bitch," repeated the other one, following.

The woman rolled her eyes and glanced at Jacob. "Sorry, didn't mean to jump in. I'm sure you guys had it all sorted until he started eyeballing me."

"Don't pretend you didn't enjoy pulling both fandom and football on him, just a little bit," Jacob said. "And by the way, hi, Aunt Lydia."

She grinned. "Maybe just a little. What's for lunch?"

Chapter Twelve

Jacob ordered an Expecto Pastrami, and Lydia got the Howl's Moving Casserole. The elven warrior insisted on buying her a Game of Scones dessert as well before leaving them. "You didn't have to come," Jacob said as they started toward the hotel doors.

"I know."

Jacob hesitated and then said, "But I appreciate the thought."

"I really don't mean to step on your toes. It's not that I didn't think you could handle it. It's just, sometimes it's easier if you don't have to be distracted and think through all the legal stuff on your own."

Jacob threw her a sideways look. "And you wanted to look for that FFVII figure."

"The fully-poseable Cloud Strife with the intricately-detailed scale Hardy Daytona motorbike? Possibly." She took a bite of her pasta.

Lydia was only fifteen years older than Jacob, but she was his aunt and legal guardian. She was also at least two points cooler than any attorney had the right to be, even according to his friends, but most of them didn't know how grateful Jacob was to her. If not for Lydia's willingness to take on the family tooth and nail, Jacob would be living a very different life. Instead, he had a normal school career and a good chance at his detective dream, not to mention a moderately healthy trust fund for emergencies.

If Lydia worried at all over him, it was only because of how fiercely they had fought to make this life, and she wouldn't let it slip away from him. He could hardly fault her for that — and she usually stayed out of the way even while she kept her eye on things.

"Aunt Lydia," he said, "I should probably warn you. There's been some video and stuff showing up around the con—"

"Hold on," she said. "What is that?"

In the corner, flanked by doors opening onto each street, stood a robot of gleaming white plastic, about nine feet tall. Jacob considered. "Looks like a giant robot," he said with deliberately flat accuracy. "I don't know which one."

Lydia slowed, and as they watched the robot, surrounded by three spotters, began to fold in upon itself. As it knelt and inverted, wheels appeared, and a tail, and a spike where a hood ornament might appear, if the construct could be called a car.

"Wow. It really transforms."

"We've got some great costumes here this year," Jacob said. "I've seen some really good stuff already."

"I wonder what kind of mileage he gets? Maybe I should upgrade." She looked around. "Man, seems like such a happy cool place. Hard to believe there was a homicide here."

"Two."

She turned to stare at him. "What?"

"Since I texted you, they found another body. Same cause of death, arsenic poisoning via food."

"Arsenic? Did I miss a trip back to 1913 or something?" She shook her head. "Same food?"

"Not sure."

"Same time?"

"No. The first one was last night, and we saw the other in Con Ops this morning. She died in the hotel bar later."

Lydia raised a tapered eyebrow. "The hotel bar?"

"It wasn't open; she was just waiting there to meet with the con chair. But she was going to be waiting a while, because we were helping him avoid her."

"Yipes. Bad romance?"

"Oh, no way. She was a corporate sponsor, and she was giving him a hard time about the con. I saw her yesterday, yelling at him in front of everyone because of a typo in the program guide. Which, to be fair, was in her company name — but it wasn't worth that level of drama."

"So is this con chair maybe a person of interest?"

"Heh," said Jacob. "I'm sure he is, but he'll have to take a number. Sorry, Aunt Lydia, but I kind of get the feeling that no one is upset about her. Shocked, yes, but not sad."

"Ah."

"So Dead-Laura was going to be hard, because there was just no context to it at all. But Valerie's going to be hard because, as far as I can pick up, she made a lot of enemies."

"Dead-Laura?" repeated Lydia. "Don't they teach you how not to be callous?"

"Oh, no, I didn't mean — her name was Tasha something. That was her costume, the dead Laura from *American Gods*, and she was doing this thing where she was gradually decaying over the weekend, like the character."

"Oh," said Lydia. "That's actually kind of cool. And sad."

Jacob's phone buzzed in his pocket. It was a text from Sam. *Audition in ten minutes. I'm starting to get nervous. Tell me something calming.*

Aunt Lydia just verbally trashed two jocks who were picking on a Helm's Deep elf.

That's really cool, but you have a weird understanding of "calming."

"Sam's going in for her audition in a few minutes," Jacob said aloud.

Lydia drew out her own phone. "Ooh, I'll tell her to break a leg." She finished the text and followed Jacob into Con Ops.

"Back from lunch," he announced. "Is Daniel around?"

"He's next door," Rita said. "You need help with something?"

"What? Oh, no. This is my Aunt Lydia. I just wanted to introduce them."

"I'll meet him later, if that's okay," Lydia said. "Can I go catch Sam's audition?"

"Sure, it's just down the hall in Main Programming. Here, take a program guide. Also, you can use the mobile app, which will have all the updates as things change."

"Do things change a lot?"

"Not a lot, but it happens. Panelist gets sick, someone doesn't show up, people suggest it's not a good idea to run a game of Murder when two people are dead. Scan this QR code, it's a free app."

"You'll need a badge," Rita said. "All the rooms have badge checks at the door."

"Even if she's just going to support a friend?" Jacob didn't really expect her to concede, but he asked anyway.

"Sorry, them's the rules. Vince was really adamant about not comping badges this year."

"It's cool," said Lydia. "I'll want to get into the dealer hall later, anyway. How much?"

She opted for the weekend pass instead of the Saturday-only badge — "in case I want to come back tomorrow" — and headed out the door.

"Hey, Jacob!" Jessica appeared, leaning over the pass-through counter. "Tag my sword for me?"

She'd changed into a pirate costume. He took the rapier, checked the edge — non-metallic and blunt — measured it, and tagged it. "I need to check the pistol, too."

She passed it to him. "Even though it's not remotely modern?"

"Any firearm replica, sorry." He turned it over. "No orange tip, Jessica? Really?"

She turned up a palm. "For an eighteenth-century gun? I didn't think it was likely anyone would mistake it for the real thing."

"Not my rules, sorry." He handed it back. "You can borrow some orange paint and tip it, or you can leave it in the room. But if Con Aid sees you with it untagged, they'll confiscate it." He glanced at the bin below the counter. "And they've been doing that all weekend, looks like."

She nodded. "I'll put it up before I head to Sam's audition. Oh, check this out." She swiped several times on her phone and held it out to him. "Look how the Trek pics were coming out, before they moved the crew. No depth of field, so it looks like the Ponies are right behind them. See that Rarity behind Captain Kirk? Like a Pony shoulder angel conscience or something. And this one, it's like the Ponies are high-fiving because Applejack is giving Spock bunny ears." She laughed.

"That's funny," Jacob said, mostly to be polite. "Sorry about the pistol. Tell Sam to be awesome."

"That's okay. I should have known, and I will. See ya." She headed off again.

Jacob looked at the schedule on the wall. "Is Daniel doing interviews?"

"If that's what you want to call it."

Jacob left Con Ops and went down to the staff suite, now empty of all refreshment but bottled water and canned soft drinks. Daniel was speaking to another officer, in more traditional uniform. "Oh, hello, Jacob. Come and meet Detective Martin."

"Anne Martin," she said with a smile, extending a hand. "Daniel says we'll be seeing you soon."

"I hope so."

There was a knock at the door, and Christopher Adams leaned in. "Hello? Is this where I should meet someone, to, you know, answer questions?"

"Come in," Detective Martin called. Her friendly smile shifted from Jacob to Christopher as she moved to pull out a chair for him. "Yes, please."

Christopher looked uncomfortable as he sat. "Paul the Programming DH told me you'd want to see me. He said everyone who saw Valerie this morning needed to talk to you."

"That's right. But this is just a preliminary interview, you know. If you'd like to wait and speak when counsel is present, that's fine, of course. No one is being charged at this time, we're just trying to get a handle on who all is even around here." Detective Martin had a soothing, dependable voice, and Jacob found himself liking her even across the room. He hoped he could develop a style like hers.

"Right. But I don't need counsel. I mean, there's no reason to need counsel for this." Christopher Adams blew out his breath. "This is just — really nerve-wracking, you know? I mean, we weren't friends, but...."

"Trust me, I understand. It's never easy. But that's why we have to do this." She glanced at Daniel and Jacob. "Would you prefer to speak privately?"

"I'm probably not going to say anything that's a big secret, so I guess it doesn't matter."

"All right, then. I'm going to make some notes, but again, this is just to help us get our bearings. It doesn't mean anything more than that right now."

He nodded.

"Can you please explain your connection to MEGAN!ME and Valerie Kimberton?"

Christopher pursed his lips. "We weren't business partners."

"Can you elaborate?"

"We were supposed to have a joint project, but it didn't happen. I was approached by Eddie Thomas, of FunFilms, to do a web series — part industry reviews, part previews, part interviews, part comedy, lots of things. I would host it, as the Terra Vista Ranger. That's my persona, see?"

It wasn't apparent whether Detective Martin did see, but she dutifully made note of it.

"Eddie was a cool guy. We talked out a deal, and I was supposed to prep a first season and FunFilms would buy it and stream it. It was going to be something really cool; Eddie wanted me to cover other companies' stuff, not just FunFilms, so it would be a pretty even-handed view."

"How does that relate to Ms. Kimberton?"

"Eddie got sick. Stomach cancer. He's doing okay now, I hear, but he ended up selling FunFilms, and MEGAN!ME snapped it up."

"Including your show?"

"Well, that's the thing. When the deal happened, Eddie told me MEGAN!ME wanted the show, too, and that it would be largely unaffected. I waited, but I didn't hear anything. And then a few months ago, I emailed to say that the season was wrapped, we were just waiting for the new logos to replace the FunFilms logos, and that MEGAN!ME already had a few good product reviews in the season, and where did they want delivery?"

The officer frowned, guessing where this was going. "When was this?"

"I got the response on April fourth. Not going to forget that any time soon. It was from Valerie, the first time I'd heard of her or from her. She said MEGAN!ME had decided not to pick up my show." Christopher didn't succeed in masking his bitterness.

"What about the deal with FunFilms?"

"Eddie told me that Dan Peters, the MEGAN!ME CEO, really liked the idea and was excited about it. But the contracts never mentioned my show, which I guess Eddie missed or just plain forgot to check after they said it was a go. He was really sick, I guess I can't blame him. But I guess we were both stupid."

Detective Martin gave him a sympathetic smile. "Love many, trust few. I'm sorry it didn't work out. What happened?"

"As far as I can tell, from talking to Eddie and asking around, Dan Peters was on board with it until Valerie took a stand. She said it was bad business to support anything which mentioned other companies' catalogs and titles."

"And they took her advice?"

Christopher scowled. "I asked a friend in Famion — they were bought out last year, but some of the staff stayed for MEGAN!ME — if she knew anything about it, and she'd heard that Valerie had a pet project of her own she wanted to do, a sort of fake video blog by a cute mascot character talking up various MEGAN!ME titles." He shook his head. "Which is all kinds of stupid. First, people want real interaction, not an animated character giving them sales pitches. And second, how is a hyper-cute little mascot going to sell *Blood Drive* and other mature-audience titles? It'd be really limiting — or else it would send the wrong message to parents about the titles and draw a lot of complaints. I had completely different sets and different costume accessories for each bracket, to keep everything straight."

Detective Martin nodded.

"Anyway, my friend heard a rumor in the company that Valerie was having her sister do the design for the *chibi*."

Detective Martin held up a finger. *"Chibi?"*

"Uh, it's a little, super-cute thing. Comes from the Japanese for *small*. Generally a little, disproportionate, hyper-cute character." He held up his key chain and pointed to a cartoonish Captain America dangling from it. "Comes in all flavors."

She nodded. "And it was thought that Valerie was having her sister do the design?"

"That's what my friend heard."

"And what's your friend's name?"

"I don't think I should tell you. She probably shouldn't have been talking to me about it, you know? Do I have to tell you?"

"Maybe later." Detective Martin closed her notebook. "That's all for now, Mr. Adams. But please don't leave the con without checking in with us, okay? In case we have any more questions."

When Christopher had gone, Detective Martin looked dubiously at Daniel. "So let me get this straight: we have a suspect whose motive would have been, his job was threatened by a stuffed animal?"

Daniel shrugged. "Some people take these things very seriously. But I have to agree with you, it doesn't seem the killing thing to do."

Martin looked down at her notes. "This whole thing's a mess. So far I've got one guy who was on a business trip to Beijing until two days ago, a woman who says the deceased had a bleak aura and probably invited dark forces, and now a professional rivalry with a cutesy animal." She wrote more, flipping pages and drawing arrows.

"Any likely faces?" asked Daniel.

"Groene has money issues, and frankly, money's a much better motive than a stuffed animal. Let's look and see if he could have benefited financially from Kimberton's death. Who knows, maybe she was bringing in a nephew to replace him as a voice actor, if that's really how she was inclined to work." She drew her phone and photographed her notes. She caught Jacob watching. "People talk more when there isn't a recorder or when you don't take a lot of notes," she explained. "So take basic notes and fill them in after they're gone. And an app which reads handwriting and makes them all searchable is worth its weight in good wine."

"What about Tasha Kurlansky?" asked Daniel. "Even if someone had a financial motive to kill Valerie, killing an unrelated cosplayer wouldn't help. It would just double the chances of being caught."

"Maybe he thought it would be camouflage? Distract from the motive by looking like random killings."

"In which case, he might not think two bodies is enough."

They looked at the empty catering tables around them. "The food court staff were supposed to be checking their kitchens."

"Do they even know what to look for?" Jacob put in. "Do we know what to tell them to look for?"

Daniel sighed. "A bag of white powder. Man, that could be anything, from cocaine to anthrax to MSG."

"How soon will they have test results back on that baggie from this morning?"

"Not soon enough."

Chapter Thirteen

Main Programming — a series of connected hotel ballrooms — had been modified for the auditions, with a black-curtained makeshift booth at the front of the room and a table and chairs on the stage. Within the curtains Sam could see an over-sized microphone, shielded by a filter, and a camera aimed down on the interior.

Lots of cons had acting or voice acting workshops or demos, and some had contests or "auditions," but most of the latter were simply filler to occupy con attendees. This one was different, however. It was still a fun event for the con, but professionals Mickey Groene, Ryan Brazil, and Sandra Shark were commenting on each entry. Most significant, however, was that each participant's attempts would be recorded, and the winner of today's contest would have this mini-reel forwarded to TruCast, who would select one voice actor from the pool of winners, taken from a dozen such contests at cons across the country, to invite for a minor role and further auditions.

It wasn't a traditional or likely path to success, but it was a potential shortcut, and the only risk was receiving an *American Idol* style dress-down in front of the con. Sam was willing to hazard that.

She had signed up for the contest almost the moment registration had opened, and she arrived a few minutes early, clutching a warm green tea and honey in a textured paper cup. She had brought the tea and honey from home and brewed it in the hotel room.

Two techs were tweaking the microphone and camera, calling back and forth from the AV station, and finally seemed satisfied. More hopefuls were filtering into the chairs, marked with a "reserved for contestants" printed sheet, and friendly, excited chatter began.

Sam eyed them. There were a few who looked serious, but about half she guessed were just here for some fun at the con, not intent on a career launch. She sipped her tea.

Onstage, the three voice actors were making their way to the table. All carried a beverage: Mickey Groene had a steel bottle, Ryan Brazil had a Starbucks cup, and Sandra Shark had a plastic bottle of water.

"You look pretty serious," said a voice beside her.

Sam glanced to her left and saw a blue-green Mole, his multi-colored antennae curling forward over his head. "Sorta. That is, I'd like to actually go into voice acting, so I want to do well today."

He nodded. "Me too. I'm majoring in theater, but they don't have a voice track." He stuck out his hand. "I'm Katnak."

"Sam. Samantha, really, but that takes too long to say."

"Using your real name? Ooh, edgy." He grinned.

Behind them, the ballroom was filling with spectators. Sam took another sip of her tea, its warmth radiating down her throat. Her phone buzzed, and she glanced down to see one more text from Jacob. *You can rock this.*

Someone else was on the stage now. "Hi, everybody. If you're here to see some great amateur voice acting, this is the place! Contestants, make sure you're checked in with Mary there with the clipboard, and we'll be getting started in just a short minute. In the meantime, let me introduce our professional panel."

Katnak rose and went to speak to Mary, along with a number of other participants. Sam had been the first.

"And Ryan will be voicing Nega Carson in the upcoming *Mega-Nega Racetrap*, which hits Playstation next — May, is it, Ryan? You don't know? They just hand you a mic and send you checks, you don't do the marketing, right." The MC laughed. "And then we have Sandra Shark."

"I do the girl characters," she said with a wave.

Because "female" is a character class, rang Jessica's indignant voice in Sam's head, and she smiled a little.

"Okay, are we ready to get started? For the audience, this is how it's going to work: we'll call a contestant into the booth. We'll close the curtain for sound quality, since we are recording these for TruCast, but you see the camera over the top here? Everything will be projected live onto the giant screens behind me. So you'll get to see every facial contortion, every blush, every tic these guys have to offer."

The crowd chuckled.

"We'll give them a character profile and a line, and they'll each have several characters to read. Our professionals will comment, but you the audience are encouraged to scream and cheer for what you like, okay?"

Katnak was called first. He went up to the booth, his multi-colored antenna bobbing as he walked. *This is the only job interview where it doesn't matter at all what you look like,* mused Sam with a private laugh.

Katnak took the page of lines and went into the curtained booth. The interior was projected onto the giant screens, and he waved at the camera.

"Okay," said the MC, "your first role is... You are a high school student who has just discovered that you possess a superpower."

Katnak looked at the sheet and laughed.

"Give it to us when you're ready."

Katnak took a breath, leaned toward the mic, and breathed in a perfect Keanu Reeves impression, "Whoa."

The audience laughed and clapped.

"Okay, good! For your next line, you're a mad scientist, just about to complete your world domination project when suddenly the doorbell rings. Play it for laughs."

Katnak nodded, studying the page. He closed his eyes for a moment, and then he unleashed on the mic, one arm holding the page and the other gesticulating as he shouted. "What, *what?* Seriously, what now? Why do I even have a doorbell on a remote mountain stronghold? Memo, disable that thing."

The audience liked this one, too. Sam clapped, trying to still the tendril of anxiety stirring within her.

"Nice, nice. Now, last one: you're a Marine, and the helicopter carrying your childhood friend who signed up with you has just been shot down. You're watching it fall and running toward the crash site."

Sam tightened her fists. This was the hard stuff.

On the screens and inside the booth, Katnak appeared similarly anxious. "Okay," he said, almost to himself, as he stared at the script page. He tested the words, running through them silently, and then he took a deep breath and licked his lips. "Noooooooooooo! Sam! Hold on, Sammy, I'm coming! I'm coming!"

It wasn't great scripting, but that wasn't Katnak's fault, and his delivery had a rawness to it that appealed. The crowd cheered, Sam included.

Katnak exited the booth and waved to everyone, and then he went up to the stage to hear the panelists' impressions.

They were brief. "Your first two, there was nothing really wrong with them," said Mickey, "but they were a bit derivative."

"That's good when a director wants a riff on something," said Ryan, "but you want to try for originality more."

"But your third one," Sandra said, "that had some potential. It wasn't a great line, but you put a lot into it."

The others nodded. "Third was your best, definitely."

"Thank you," said Katnak. "I appreciate your thoughts."

He returned to sit beside Sam. "Sorry for screaming your name like that," he whispered. "Especially as we've only just met."

She cast a darkly incredulous look at him and turned back to the stage.

"Sorry," he said again, "that was uncalled for. Really."

"You're right," she said, "but apologizing helps."

"Nervous energy," he said. "I always get the shakes right after I get off a stage or something. Worse after than before. It's weird."

The next contestant entered the booth and was given the role of a cheery alien observing human children at play.

"I freak out before," Sam said, "and then I spend three hours afterward rehashing everything I should have done differently."

He laughed.

The reading contestant giggled through two of her three lines, and for the third, a parent looking down at a child's grave, she broke off laughing and said she couldn't do it. The next contestant, however, was pretty good, and the audience cheered her as she exited the booth.

Sam's name was called about halfway through, by which time her hands were sweaty and her breath shortening. That was bad for voice work, and she tried to take slow, deep breaths as she approached the booth.

Someone was cheering from the audience, and she turned to see Lydia with her hands funneling a whoop. She smiled and waved. To the side, Zach and Jessica were clapping and shouting encouragement too.

Surely the script would grow damp and saggy in her wet hands. She took the page without looking at the MC and went into the booth.

She did most of her voice practice in her car as she drove, private and ever available. The makeshift booth wasn't too different in size. Sam drew a deep breath, letting her diaphragm and lower abdomen expand.

"Okay, first up, you're surprised by the appearance of your explorer friend who has been missing for months."

Sam looked at the script. Seriously? How could anyone work with this clunker of a line?

But silence stretched outside the booth. She curled her fingers. "Tell us how you escaped from Devil's Island, Randolph."

There wasn't much sound from the audience outside. She wasn't sure if that meant that they didn't like it, or if she wasn't supposed to hear much of them inside the deadening curtains. But how could they have liked a line like that, no matter how it was read?

"Okay. Next up, you're a successful actress, about forty, talking to a friend about your divorce."

This one had more possibilities. Sam thought a moment, tested a breezy tone in her mind, and then loftily said, "Oh, Doug, I'm far too busy to be upset. I have my broadcasts, my fan mail, my detailed plans for how to dispose of Jeff's body...."

The audience liked this one, she could hear. She smiled and gave the camera a thumbs-up. They liked that, too.

"Very good! Now, for your final role, you are a parent who has just heard your child having a horrific nightmare. Come in and gently wake him."

Sam's stomach clenched. She had done lots of heroic voices in her car, lots of challenges, lots of sarcasm and snark. She hadn't practiced much maternal.

She stared at the page, her thumb marking the third set of lines. *Come on, Sam. Think gentle.* The camera stared at her, waiting. Who could be a touchstone for this? Who had a kind, child-friendly voice, that wouldn't sound all creepy and predatory?

Mr. Rogers. There was no one kinder and friendlier and more soothing than Mr. Rogers, and if they didn't like it, well, she didn't want to work in an industry which rejected Fred Rogers.

She closed her eyes against the camera and thought of a gentle man in a sweater. She opened her eyes and found the words marked by her thumb. "Wait, little one, hush. It's all right; there's nothing in the dark. Only me, and I'm here to sit with you and watch the night go by."

It wasn't the kind of monologue to inspire wild cheering, but they cheered anyway, if politely. Sam exhaled and opened the curtain, heading to the stage to hear the voice actors' feedback.

Mickey spoke first. "Man, that first line, I felt for you. Who wrote this stuff? I'm sorry. But you did the best you could with it."

"It's totally a female line," Sandra stage-whispered, and they all laughed. "Like, Ooh, hero-guy, tell me how you were amazing so I can be amazed."

"I guess you could put a lot of sarcasm into it," mused Ryan. "Lots of eye-rolling? Would that help?"

"Not really," said Mickey. "But you pulled it through — what's your name?"

"Sam."

"Sam. You gave it what you had, which is all anyone can ask. After that...."

"After that is when she brought the snark," said Sandra. "Which was good."

"And it was at the opposite end of the spectrum from the last line, which was all warm and fuzzy," Mickey said. "So that's good range."

"Good job," Ryan summed up. "Keep working."

"Thank you," said Sam, and as she returned to her seat she wondered if she should have said more. It seemed kind of flat.

When she sat down, though, Katnak gave her a big grin. "I should probably hate you," he said, "but that was pretty good."

"Hate me?"

"Because I was figuring it was going to be me and that guy who did the goat-man, and now I've got to beat him if I want to be in the top two."

Sam felt her face pull into a wide smile. "I don't think it was quite that definitive, but thanks."

Her phone buzzed with texts from Lydia and Jessica. *Awesome, you rocked it,* and, *Sweet pipes, girlfriend.*

She didn't hear the next couple of contestants, as she was replaying her lines over and over in her mind. *Leave it alone,* she told herself. *Nothing you can change about it now. Just wait for it.* But her internal playback kept going.

Chapter Fourteen

"Got the toxicology analysis back on that powder," Detective Martin announced as she entered the staff suite. "Initial, anyway, it was a rush job. It's definitely some sort of arsenate or — oh, hold on." She withdrew her phone and read aloud, "Consistent with lead hydrogen arsenate."

"So it's arsenic," Daniel said. "We really are back in the days of Agatha Christie and inheritance powder. But what's lead hydrogen arsenic?"

"Arsenate," corrected Detective Martin mildly. "Apparently it's a pesticide, or was."

Jacob pulled out his phone. "The internet to the rescue," he said. "Lead hydrogen arsenate, right? Wow, it's kind of a hot topic online...."

"I don't really care about what 4chan has to say about it," Daniel interrupted. "We've got a homicide involving it. Two homicides."

"We'll know more when they've got a final analysis," Detective Martin said. "In the meanwhile, it's creepy enough. How did a bag of it get into the kitchen? Was it supposed to go into the food for everyone?"

"Hold on," Jacob said. "Here's a petition to the FDA to stop import of Chinese apples and apple concentrate for juices, due to high arsenic content."

"You think that's relevant?" asked Daniel.

"It might be," Jacob said. "The petition site says that arsenic pesticides are mostly illegal in the US but are still used in China. And wasn't there somebody who just got back from China?"

Daniel looked at Jacob. "And you're suggesting that he bought an illegal pesticide there and brought it back to use as a murder weapon?"

Jacob hesitated. "Well, when you say it that way…."

"It's worth making a note of," Daniel said, surprising Jacob. "Weirder things have happened."

"Who just got back from China?" Detective Martin ran a search on her phone. "Oh, right, that's Hammer. Greg Hammer."

Jacob stared. "Greg Hammer? But… why would he?"

"He did have a connection with the victim," Detective Martin said. "Not close, but there was a business relationship."

"No way," Jacob said. "Hammer has fame and fortune already. What would be his motive?"

"Money and passion, that's the standard line," said Daniel. "But there can be other things, too."

Jacob screwed up his face. "Passion with Valerie Kimberton? I mean, yeah, she wasn't bad-looking, but…."

"But sometimes she might talk out loud and ruin the effect," Daniel said. "Still, no accounting for taste."

"Not Greg Hammer. He's an artist. A really good artist."

"Really good artists have weird quirks."

Jacob looked bleakly at the schedule on the wall. *Not Greg Hammer.* "Still, I think we ought to know more about it first."

Daniel raised an eyebrow. "Do you happen to have an expert handy on toxic pesticides in the food supply?"

Jacob blew out his breath. "No, but — hold on, yes, I

might." He drew out his phone. "Let me text my favorite social justice warrior."

Jessica might not know much about arsenic and pesticides, but she would certainly know who would.

It was nearing the end of the allotted time for the voice acting contest, and they had two participants left to go. Sam kept glancing at the clock on her phone. Would they have time to review and declare winners? They had all the participants' email addresses, but if they had to wait....

The last contestant was a girl in her mid-teens. She was good, with a solid classic horror scream which probably turned some heads in the corridor outside. But Sam wondered if she were too young to be able to take advantage of the TruCast offer. And she sounded young, not much vocal range yet.

"And that's our last entry," announced the MC. "I think our judges have been making notes as we went, so we'll just give them a few minutes...."

Beside Sam, Katnak crossed his fingers and gave her a grin. "You and me. Then goat-man. But you and me first."

A mini-reel sent in from a winner, even a minor winner, would stand out from the dozens or hundreds of submissions TruCast received each week. She was good, she knew she was. She just needed that tiny boost to catch someone's eye and prove it....

Two men in jeans and black t-shirts appeared to bend over the voice actors' table, pushing a sheet of paper back and forth. Sandra and Ryan seemed to disagree on something, and then Mickey whispered and they all laughed.

"Are we ready?" prompted the MC. "Do we have our winners?"

One of the black t-shirt men nodded.

"Let me just remind our audience that these contestants are competing not only against each other for fame and glory, but against contestants at other conventions for a chance to be considered for an actual voice role by TruCast," he said with artificial excitement. "So, whose recording gets sent?"

They pushed the sheet at Mickey, who looked surprised and then leaned toward his microphone. "Um, we have our two winners. They are, Gary 'Katnak' Osterman, and Juan Diaz."

Katnak pumped his fist and hissed, "Yes!" In the next row, the man who'd done the goat-man impression leapt to his feet and cheered.

Sam swallowed and offered Katnak a hand. "Congratulations."

He shook it. "Man, I'm sorry. You were good."

"Thanks."

Katnak and the other winner went forward to claim their certificates and take care of the TruCast paperwork, and Sam rose and started back to the doors. Jessica and Zach met her in the aisle. "Robbed," Zach declared. "Totally robbed."

"Don't be unfair," she told him. "Those guys were pretty good, too."

"It's because there were four men and only one woman judging," Jessica said. "You got pushed aside."

"I don't think that's what happened." Sam sighed. "That first line… I should have done something to jazz it up somehow. Nobody writes something that flat without hanging a lampshade on it. I should have played it for laughs."

"You did fine," Zach said. "Don't beat yourself up over nothing."

Lydia worked her way through the exiting crowd and threw an arm about Sam. "You were awesome. And robbed. And awesome."

"Told you," said Zach.

"You okay?" asked Jessica. "Need some frozen yogurt or anything?"

Sam laughed. "I didn't win a contest," she said. "It's not like I failed a class or found a breakup note. It's cool."

"I ran out on Jacob, so I'm going to check in with him," Lydia said. "But you were great." She headed down the hallway.

"We're heading to a Marvel Cinematic Universe versus comics panel," Zach said. "Want to come?"

"Nah, I was thinking about the Ubisoft preview," Sam said. "Catch you later."

She hadn't gone far when someone caught up to walk beside her, and she recognized Ryan Brazil in his tight green polo shirt. "Excuse me," he said, "what was your name?"

"I'm Sam."

"Sam, I thought you were fantastic," he said. "It was that clunker of a first line that really sold you, I think. You gave it all you had, really professional."

"Thanks."

"You looked pretty intense in there. Are you serious about voice acting?"

She shrugged. "I guess. If you count that I've wanted to be a voice actress since I was eight."

He laughed. "Yeah, you're serious. Listen," he continued, "I really wanted to pick you, but I got outvoted. But I'm willing to speak for you, Sam. I think you've got talent."

"Really?"

"Really. And if I get a chance to mention someone for an unfilled part, I'd be happy to put your name in — if that's all right."

"Sure," Sam said, trying not to grin stupidly. A personal recommendation from an established actor would go much further than a minor contest win. "Sure, that'd be fine. Actually, I'd really appreciate it."

"Great. I don't suppose you have a card?" He shook his head. "No, probably not. Not yet, anyway. But here." He drew out his phone. "You can just friend me on Facebook and we'll be able to stay in touch that way. Ryan Brazil, see like this." He tilted his phone so that she could see the screen.

"Sure, thanks." She pulled out her own phone from her messenger bag and searched for him in Facebook. "Here, I'm liking your page."

"No, not the fan page — my personal page. So we can actually talk."

"Oh, okay. Thanks. Here you are, sending friend request now."

He refreshed and tapped the screen. "And, friends!"

"Great. Thank you. Really, thank you."

"My pleasure, Sam. We'll be in touch."

"Thanks."

Ryan went off in another direction, and Sam started down the hall again, smiling to herself. This was better than winning. This was networking, a personal recommendation, a straighter shot to where she wanted to be. Her talent had been recognized.

Frozen yogurt didn't sound bad, after all — not as consolation, but as celebration. She changed her course and headed for the food court. The Ubisoft panel probably didn't have much that she didn't already know anyway.

The food court was eerily transformed. A number of attendees were scattered among the tables, but all the food counters were closed, barriers down or lights out. Inside several of the restaurant fronts, uniformed police and at least one K-9 team were moving in the kitchens, while employees stood outside the counters, watching.

A few paces away, a Solid Snake from the *Metal Gear* franchise was scrolling on his phone. Sam looked at him. "What happened?"

"Huh? Oh, food's shut down. Hotel food, food court food, all of it. Somebody found something. There's a message on the mobile app, says that the con is working to get more food options ASAP." He pointed. "There's still the food trucks outside that way, though I think some of them were starting to run out of things."

"Thanks." Sam reflected that she hadn't had lunch yet, and she probably should hit the food trucks before they were completely sold out.

She thumbed open the con's mobile app as she walked. An alert message popped up immediately.

> *As you may have heard, the hospitality services at our host hotel and the food court have been suspended. This is due to the utmost caution as we assist in the investigation of two food-related deaths. It is not known that the victims ingested hotel or food court meals, but to be absolutely safe, all hotel and food court kitchens are being examined closely. We understand that this is a major inconvenience, and we apologize, but we hope you can understand our desire to keep our attendees safe. We are working to find alternate*

"Oh, no." They wouldn't have shut down the kitchens, not with so many thousands of hungry attendees willing to pay for meals, unless there was something suspicious about them.

She got in line at a truck, noticing that half the blackboard menu was already scratched out. While she waited, she sent a message to Jacob. *Just read the message about the food. Yipes! Things okay? I'm about to eat at a food truck. Is that safe?*

After a moment, he replied. *Food trucks should be fine. We are really short-handed though. You busy?*

I can help out for a bit. Coming as soon as I grab lunch.

She ordered a vegetarian chili in a Bread Pirate Roberts bowl, and then she started back into the hotel, spooning hot chili into her mouth. It was a good day to be wearing a comfortable and mobile costume like Barnstorming Betty, she reflected.

She was tearing the piratical bread bowl into bite-sized pieces by the time she reached Con Ops. "Hey, I'm Sam. Jacob said you needed some help?"

The con chair looked up. "Do you have a car?"

"What? Uh, yeah, we shared a ride here."

"Fantastic. We're buried here. We've got some volunteers to help out, but no one had wheels." He turned and pointed to Micky Groene, surprising Sam. "Can you two run and pick up food?"

"For the entire con?" asked Sam. "That's gonna be a heck of a drive-through order."

"Head south, there's a major shopping center there,

and I'm pretty sure I saw a wholesale club as I was coming in," Vince said. "Here's the membership card, that'll get you in. Buy energy bars, canned drinks, cup ramen, those individual microwave meals that don't have to be refrigerated, whatever you can find. Bring them back here, and the hotel is going to set up tables where we can sell the stuff. As long as it's all pre-packaged, we don't need a restaurant license or inspection. Got it?"

"Got it," Mickey said. "How do we pay for it?"

Vince took another card from his wallet. "Here's the con's Visa. For the love of Kirk, don't lose that."

"How much do we get?" asked Sam.

"We have eight thousand people here," Vince said. "Some of them will bail and go home, and some will order in, but there's not a lot of options around here. Hotel convention space was pretty self-sufficient until it was shut down. Get everything you can, and we'll return what we don't use."

"Right. Everything that fits into a Geo Metro."

Vince's mouth twisted into a tired smile. "You can make two trips."

"I'm kidding. We packed four people in for the weekend, and three of us are cosplayers. When I need to fit something in there, the thing's practically a TARDIS." She smiled at Mickey. "You ready?"

Chapter Fifteen

"I really liked your reading in the contest," Mickey said without preamble as he fastened the seat belt. "It was nice work."

Sam started the Metro and eased backward. "Thanks."

"I gave you some bonus points for that first line. What a beast. It was an awful line, but you were very professional about it."

Sam smiled. "That's about the nicest thing you can say for that, yeah."

He laughed. "If it's any consolation, I wanted to give you the prize. Don't get me wrong, the other guys were good, but goat-man had two great lines. You had two great lines and a really good effort at saving a sinking ship."

"Well, that's good to know. Guess I just needed to convince Sandra, huh?"

"What? No, Sandra loved you. You were her number one pick."

A pedestrian started across the street, against the lights and without looking at the traffic, and Sam hit the brakes. "Yipes! Crazy people. I swear, he didn't even look this way."

"Crazy," agreed Mickey. "Anyway, don't let it get you down. You should definitely send a demo, even if you didn't win."

"I will."

They found the wholesale store, and the Con Job card got them inside. Sam got a shopping cart, and they started for the dry goods section. "We're just going to clean them out," Mickey said, sweeping several cases of granola bars into the cart. "In fact, you'd better grab another cart."

"I'll get one of the flatbeds instead."

When they had stacked both the flatbed cart and the shopping cart beyond safe limits, they wrestled the goods to the front of the store. "Wow," said the cashier. "You must be having one serious party."

"You should see the other guy," said Mickey. "Oh, wait, that line doesn't work here." He pulled out the Con Job credit card. "Put it all on the plastic."

She rang up the dozens of boxes and then swiped the card. She frowned. "Sorry, it says this one is over limit."

"How far over the limit?" Sam asked. "Could we put a couple of boxes back?"

"No, not like that," the cashier said. "Like, this card is no good. It says to hold the card, which means it hasn't been paid or is stolen."

"It's not stolen," Mickey said hastily. "But this is an emergency use in the middle of the convention, so it might not have been paid off." He looked at Sam. "I don't suppose you carry large quantities of cash, do you?"

She glanced at the register. "Not like that, no."

Mickey sighed. "Try this." He pulled another credit card from his wallet. "This one's my own, so I'll need two copies of the receipt, please."

"Sure." She ran the card. "Um, same thing."

Mickey swore. "Try this one."

She took it, looking skeptical, and swiped it.

Sam dialed Jacob. As the phone rang, the cashier looked at Mickey and shook her head. "No good. I'd like to help you out, but...."

"Hello?" said Jacob's voice from the phone.

"Jacob, are you in Ops? Or near Vince?"

"Right beside him. What's up?"

"The con credit card is overdrawn. If we pick it up, can he pay us back?"

"Hang on." She heard Jacob relaying the question.

Vince took the phone. "You're very trusting," he said. "But get the receipt, two copies if you can, and bring everything back here. You'll get reimbursed off the top of everything we make selling the food."

"Sounds good," she said. "It'll be less than we planned, because my credit limit isn't super-high."

"Just do what you can."

"We'll be back soon."

She hung up and told the cashier, "Give me just one second, I'm sorry. Mickey, can you pick out some of the less critical stuff? Whatever you think, maybe the candy bars?"

She opened her bank app and checked the available funds on her credit card, then showed the screen to the cashier. "We've got this much to work with. Tell us what we can buy."

It took a few minutes, but they were able to sort the cases and packages until they had the flatbed full of purchases and the cart full of rejects. "I'm really sorry about the trouble," Mickey said to the cashier. "Thanks for being patient with us."

"Man, you didn't cuss me out when your card was rejected," she said. "Sad to say, that already puts you ahead of some people. Like it's my fault they didn't pay their bills."

It took them more time and some creative packing, but in the end Mickey slid into the front seat and Sam wedged the remaining cases of energy bars and microwaveable macaroni and cheese between his lap and the dashboard. She eased out of the parking lot, leaning around him to see the oncoming traffic.

"Don't hit anything," Mickey said. "This would be about the most humiliating obituary ever, crushed and suffocated in convenience cheese sauce."

Sam giggled. "At least you'd be dead. I'd be charged with homicide by mac and cheese."

They loaded the food onto two luggage carts, guarded by hotel bellhops, and headed to Con Ops. "We've got food," Mickey announced. "Where does it go?"

"Great!" Vince jumped up. "The hotel's supposed to be setting up some tables in the lobby. We'll divide it up, put some at each to try to give ourselves at least a fighting chance of keeping the lines down. What do we have?"

Sam produced a receipt. "Energy bars, canned drinks, microwaveable mac and cheese — there's microwaves in the rooms — cup ramen, candy bars. Not a lot of vegan options, sorry."

"True, but most of my vegan friends travel with their own food, anyway," said Mickey. "They're probably the best off right now, laughing at us with their soy cheese bean burritos while we're flailing." He grinned.

Rita threw him a smug smile. "It was an enchilada, but yes, I had one about an hour ago."

Mickey gave her a little salute. "Always prepared."

"Rita, can you type up a price list?" Vince was scanning the receipt and typing numbers into his phone calculator. "Okay, energy bars, candy bars, and drinks are a buck each. Mac and cheese will be — hang on...."

"I know those drinks didn't cost any dollar each," said Paul. "You're going to make a killing."

Vince looked up. "For emergency rations, that's pretty reasonable — especially since they would have paid two dollars for a drink in the food court. Profit isn't illegal or unethical, and they might actually end up saving money. What was a bowl of noodles and a drink at the hotel restaurant?"

Paul shrugged. "Point."

"We need at least two staff at each table, one handling money and one managing product."

"I've got people lined up," Rita said. "We're pulling them off Registration. Reg always slows down by Saturday afternoon, and somehow I don't think we're going to get a run on badges now, anyway."

"You're probably right on that," Vince said. "And the Reg people are already cleared for handling cash, so that's good. Sam, Mickey, thank you. I'll keep this receipt, Sam, if you have another? Okay, good. As soon as we get some liquid cash, I'll reimburse you for this. Thanks for covering it."

Mickey waved. "I'm going to get back to schmoozing, but let me know if you need anything else, okay?"

"Thanks. I mean it. This was all way beyond guest duties."

"No problem, happy to help."

Sam was nearly at the door when it was pushed open and a man in hotel livery leaned inside. "A woman on floor seventeen was just attacked," he said. "Security's with her now, police are on the way. She was one of your attendees, if you want to come along."

Vince swore. "Is she okay?"

"I haven't seen her, but word is she's a little battered, but okay. Her stuff was stolen, a photography bag — pink and skulls, they say, if anyone sees it. Staff's on alert to watch for it."

"Oh, no!" breathed Sam. "That's Laser."

Chapter Sixteen

Laser had dark skin and long micro-braids pulled back from her face, which was abraded and bruising beneath the cold pack she held to her eye and cheek. She was dressed in her trademark bondage pants and a slim purple shirt. Sam and Jessica sat on either side of her. Sam had called Jessica on their way up.

Beside Laser's feet sat an enormous rolling gear bag, bright pink with white skulls pockmarked with rhinestones. A hotel security officer had just brought it in, and she was rummaging through it with one hand.

"Your name?" asked the policewoman. Detective Martin, she'd introduced herself.

"Bonnie Freeman. But pretty much everyone here knows me as Laser, for Laser Focus Photography."

"Can you describe what happened?"

"I can tell you what I know," Laser said. "I was coming back to my room, where I was going to get some energy bars and maybe take a nap before my next shoot. I've been going about eight hours so far. I took the elevator, which was full of people, but no one else got off on this floor. I was getting my key card out of my pocket when I heard footsteps, real loud and coming up real fast, and I just had time to start to turn when he hit me. Like, full on tackled me. I hit the floor, and he grabbed my hair and banged my head into the ground a couple of times. He yelled at me to stay down — I don't know that I even could have gotten up, I was really stunned — and then he got off me and kicked me in the head. Just once, I think. It took me a minute to get oriented, and when I didn't hear him I kind of sat up, and he was gone. And so was my bag."

"What happened then?"

"I went into my room. I was just really glad that he hadn't taken my room key and dragged me in there, you know? I was scared, not gonna lie. I called the front desk, they sent security up. And I have to say, they were fast, and one man, one woman. I appreciated that."

The officer nodded.

"And they called you — the police, I mean." Laser set down the cold pack so she could use both hands in the equipment bag.

Sam picked up the pack and pressed it to her head again. "You need to keep the ice on there."

"I need to see what's missing."

A security officer had discovered the abandoned bag in the vending nook, near the elevator and stair well, while covering the hotel floor for anyone suspicious. It was open and had obviously been ransacked, but the thief had left much of the contents in the bag.

"Your assailant might have hidden in the vending nook to rummage through the bag," said the police officer. "It's pretty distinctive, and he probably knew it wasn't safe to risk being seen with it."

"I knew it was Laser as soon as I heard about the bag," Sam said, one arm around her. "Half the cosplay community knows that bag. No way could he have walked it through the con without getting noticed."

"And apparently he knew that, which implies he's a member of the convention." Detective Martin made notes as she spoke. "He might have been hiding there in the nook, too, when you got off the elevator. He probably was waiting."

Laser shuddered.

"Did you see anyone else in the hall?"

"No, no one."

"Can you say what race your assailant was? What was he wearing?"

"I didn't see a thing. He took me down and then I just saw stars and carpet. I heard him, he was male, but that's it." She shuddered again. "You know how you can think super-fast when something's happening, faster than normal? I thought maybe he was the murderer, you know, who killed that cosplayer and the MEGAN!ME woman. I thought he was going to kill me."

"It's like the con is cursed," Jessica said, squeezing her. "This is insane."

"I'm very glad he didn't," said Detective Martin. "And not to discount your financial loss, Ms. Freeman, but the theft of camera equipment isn't the same as killing people. It was probably some lowlife who wants to make a quick buck reselling. I'm sorry."

"It's just such a jerk thing to do. That's my life, you know? It's going to cost me a fortune to replace. And all the pics I'd shot for the cosplayers, so they won't get them, either." She shook her head. "I'll have to refund their money. Which is totally fair, but... that was my food money for the weekend, too." Laser shook her head.

"We'll spot you," Jessica said. "We'll share pizza and there's supposed to be some food soon in the lobby, and we can get you something."

"You're lucky, as awful as it is to say it," Detective Martin said. "You got away with just some abrasions and bruising, though we'll want to get you checked out just in case."

"Yeah, don't get me wrong, I'm grateful to be as okay as I am. But I'm beyond pissed that it happened at all." She took a breath. "Which is good, because I think that's the only thing keeping me from crying right now."

"At least he didn't take everything, what with the bag being so distinctive," Sam said. "Just the most valuable stuff."

"Except that he didn't. Some of them, yeah, it's gonna flatten me to get a new camera and lenses. But some of the stuff he took is just stupid."

"What all is missing?" Detective Martin asked. "Have you gone through it all?'

"The camera body, two lenses — those are the biggest hit, money-wise — some gels, a Fong, and the zipper case of SD cards." Laser shook her head. "Which is full of stupid, because SD cards are cheap, and it was underneath the portrait lens, which he left. He had to think they were something else. I hope he's good and disappointed."

"Sometimes thieves dump worthless or less valuable goods," Detective Martin said. "There's a chance he'll toss it when he realizes it's not going to sell."

"That's a lot of trash cans to check," Laser said sadly.

Detective Martin frowned at her notes. "Can you spell Fong and tell me what it is?"

"F-O-N-G. It's a sort of diffuser."

"Laser!" Jacob came in and squatted beside the bed. "Are you okay? Oh, man, that looks awful."

"Thanks a lot," she joked feebly. "I'll be okay, though they're going to take me in and make sure my brain's not scrambled. He rang my bell a bit."

"You need to do something about this," Sam said, looking at Jacob. "Con security. This kind of thing can't happen."

Jacob gave her a pleading look. "We're Aid, not security, and you know that's for a reason. We can't police an entire building. And it's not exactly like nothing else has been going on."

"Exactly," Sam said. "Something's going on. And I know I'm being unreasonable, but people are getting hurt, and it needs to stop."

"We're working on it," said Detective Martin firmly, "doing as much as we can. Now let's focus on catching this particular toilet scrub as soon as possible. Can you think of anything else missing from the bag?"

Laser shook her head. "No. I've been going over and over in my mind. I can't think of anything else missing. He left the flashes, which are worth the most after the camera and lenses, and the beauty dish, and everything else I can think of."

"So probably not knowledgeable about photography," Detective Martin mused, "or else in a big hurry. Is there a chance it was one of the cosplayers? Stealing the cards and trying to get the pictures for free?"

"Oh, no," Laser said immediately. "I know pretty much everyone I shot this weekend, and I can't imagine any of them doing something like that."

"People can surprise you. Sad, but true."

"I know, but…. I just can't see it."

Detective Martin looked steadily at her. "Who was the last person you photographed?"

"That was FerretAngel. She was in Belldandy, OVA version. Before that was Rogue and Knight, doing Mara Jade and Boba Fett."

"Okay, but who are they really?"

"What?"

"I assume Rogue isn't what's on her driver's license."

"No. Um, Rogue is Rogue Star online, and Knight is RedKnight. They're from somewhere in the Chicago area."

"Real names?"

"I don't know. Rogue's might be Amelia something; I think I heard someone make a *Doctor Who* joke once. But I don't know last names."

"So you don't know these people's real names or where they're from, but you feel confident they wouldn't do anything illegal?"

Laser's mouth twisted. "Rogue is an accountant at a tire factory. RedKnight is an elementary school teacher, and he keeps his name on the down-low because he's worried that administration would give him a hard time if they found out he does costume stuff, which is full of stupid, but at least he's got a reason for an alias. FerretAngel lives in Missouri, has three cats, is in her second year of med school, likes vegetable pizza but can be talked into pepperoni, is afraid of spiders, used to be afraid of flying but learned some relaxation techniques to help in the air, and she's been dating this guy on and off for two years and thinks maybe she should end it permanently but is afraid he'll go a little berserk if she does. So no, it's not like I don't know these people. I just don't know their names and addresses."

Detective Martin sighed. "I see what you're saying, but—"

Jacob spoke up. "There's another reason it's pretty unlikely, and that's because Laser charges way too little for her pics. Most con photographers do."

"You did a one-hour shoot, you said." Detective Martin turned back to Laser. "You've got the shoot itself, plus processing, plus prints or digital copies. Could be hundreds in the end. My daughter got married last spring, and there's a lot of people who would steal for that kind of money."

Jacob shook his head. "Totally different market. Laser charges — what, fifty bucks a shoot, depending on the con?"

She nodded.

"And that includes processing and all the pics she deems good enough to release."

Detective Martin's jaw dropped. "But — they said you were pro. I mean, really good."

"She's crazy good," Sam said. "She shoots weddings and portraits and art shots when she's not at cons."

Laser blushed.

"But con rates are usually lower, because a lot of photographers use them to get started and a lot of attendees, especially the younger ones, don't have extra money. It's just the market. Anyway, nobody's going to steal her camera and keep her from doing the processing and from putting up photos for everyone to admire and re-post all over Facebook and Tumblr. People do this to show off their work; stealing her camera would do the exact opposite."

Detective Martin nodded and looked at Laser. "Okay, first, I need a business card. Second, we need all the details of the missing equipment, so we can distribute lists to pawn shops and the like. I presume you know all the makes and models?"

Laser slid a few screens on her phone and held up a view of Evernote. "I have all the serial numbers logged here."

"Fantastic, that will really speed things along. I wish everyone were half as organized."

A niggling sense of something important brushed at Jacob's mind. Why take the cheap SD cards but leave the valuable off-camera flashes and other equipment?

"So now I wait?" asked Laser.

Detective Martin nodded. "Yep. You get medically cleared, but then we wait."

Laser sighed. "I guess I'll wait, then. That's more than a little frustrating." She slapped her hands on her thighs.

"Where were you shooting today?" asked Jacob.

"Oh, man, all over," she said. "I did a couple of shoots in the conservatory, and then that beautiful Achenar in the side lobby, by the mosaics and fountain, and then I did a *Nightlife* shoot in an access corridor and a stairwell, for a bit of urban feel, and then an *Alice in Wonderland* in the conservatory again."

"Was anyone else in the access corridor?"

"Oh, no. We won't stay if it looks like we might be in anyone's way. That's why we get to do them at all. One guy passed us while we were setting up in the stairwell, but not during shooting. We were pretty high up, to avoid the foot traffic."

Detective Martin looked at Jacob. "Why do you ask?"

He shook his head. "Can't really explain. Just.... My friend Jessica showed me the pictures she took during the *Star Trek* shoot with some unintentional photobombs. And I thought just now, maybe something was in the background, or someone, and that's why the camera was stolen?" He gestured, trying to explain. "Because otherwise why take the time to dig out the extra SD cards? Those are cheap, especially compared to the other stuff left behind. It means somebody wanted the photos — and like Sam said, it wouldn't be any of the modeling cosplayers, who had already paid and were getting them anyway."

Detective Martin nodded. "That makes good sense. Any other potential reasons?"

Sam frowned. "Maybe someone wanted to pass off

Laser's shots as their own? Except that the cosplayers could shout that down pretty quickly, once the photos were posted. We tend to know a photographer's style. Or, and this is way out there, someone wanted to Photoshop a cosplayer into something really ugly and damaging — but seriously, I've never even heard of anything like that, and again, it'd be easy to deny. Laser's pretty known in the community, and once it's out there that her equipment was stolen, everyone would be suspicious of any weird stuff going on."

"Even the hallway pics," Laser said. "Convention center hotels are pretty distinctive — that is, they all have their own flavor of ugly furnishings we have to work around. Lots of times you can pinpoint what con a photo was taken at by the carpet and furniture, it's practically a game. No one would dare to post any of those photos taken right where they were stolen."

"Sounds like a reasonable guess, then, to leave open the possibility that the thief was just stupid — which happens a lot, actually," Detective Martin said. "But the idea that he was worried about something potentially in the background is a good one." She looked at Laser. "I don't suppose there's a chance you were using those cards that upload while you take pictures?"

Laser shook her head. "Cost a lot, and not wholly compatible with my equipment."

Jacob held up a finger to interrupt. "Laser, you let people shoot over you, right? With their phones?"

"What? Oh, definitely. Everybody likes the costumes, and I'm not worried about competing with a cell phone camera. Why?"

"I'll bet a hundred or more photos were taken over your shoulder of that CLUTCH costume alone. That's a hundred pics which might have that same something, whatever it is, in the background. What if we ask everyone to share their photos?"

"Kind of like the FBI did with the Boston Marathon suspects?"

"It wasn't quite like that, but the same idea. And then we look for anything weird in the pics." He shrugged. "It's not great, but you never know, it might turn up something."

Detective Martin considered. "Let me run it by someone above me, but yeah, maybe. How would you put the word out?"

"Oh, that's easy. Con's mobile app, the Twitter feed. Specify one upload bin. We'll get some spam and joke submissions, sure, but we'll get more legit ones."

"Work it out," said Detective Martin, "and get me the details."

Chapter Seventeen

Jacob finished typing and half-turned in the chair. "Paul? This is ready, if you approve."

Paul glanced at the screen. "This is the cops' wording?"

"Yeah, exactly. We're just helping them spread the word."

"Then we're probably covered, liability-wise, and I can't see any issues with it. You've got a photo drop already set up?"

Jacob alt-tabbed to display a Flickr page. "Not fancy, but efficient. Anyone with a Flickr account can upload straight to the 'Con Job Photo Request' group. People who aren't Flickr users can email them or use the Twitter hashtag."

"Looks good." Paul leaned over the keyboard and signed into the mobile scheduling software. "Paste it all in here, and hit Update."

The request for photos would appear on every smartphone and tablet using the mobile app. Jacob set up a new column to track the #ConJobPhotoReq hashtag in Twitter. The police would be collecting and analyzing everything, of course, but it would be interesting to track what kind of response they received.

He pulled a sheet of paper from the printer beside him and wrote, *why kill Tasha/Dead-Laura?* A couple of inches over, he wrote, *why kill Valerie K?* Ringing the two questions, he began to write short lines about the con and incidents. *Laser assaulted, robbed. CoCO in viewing rooms. Photobombs. Powder in kitchen.*

He drew a dotted line between *Laser assaulted, robbed* and *Photobombs*. There were no lines connecting any of the other items yet, just a scattering of isolated thoughts.

The door opened, and Jacob looked up as Daniel escorted, politely but firmly, someone new into Con Ops. The teen jerked away from Daniel's hand and flung himself into a folding chair, slouching with arms crossed and scowl fixed firmly. Behind them came a short woman in a *Final Fantasy VII* shirt, also with crossed arms and a furious expression. She remained standing.

"So," Daniel said, "this is probably the last chance to resolve this peaceably. Are you willing to pay for the item?"

"I already told you, I don't have it," the teen snapped. "Nobody's got two hundred bucks for a stupid statue. That's stupid."

Daniel turned to the woman, who spoke before he could. "I want to press charges."

"All right, then." He took out his phone and began dialing.

"You can't arrest me!" the boy said. "I'm an American citizen. I have rights. You're not police."

"You can be held by building security until police arrive," Daniel said evenly, the phone to his ear, "and in fact I am police. Sergeant Daniel Ratherman." He pulled the badge from his Imperial uniform jacket to display.

The kid swore.

Jacob put his eyes back on the Twitter feed — two comments and three photos already — but he could hear clearly Daniel's report of a theft from a vendor who wanted to press charges. The woman spoke again. "What will you need from me?"

"You can go on back to your booth, and we'll send someone to take a statement when they get here. Thanks, and I'm sorry about all of this."

"Some people are entitled little brats," she said, an edge to her voice. "I'm just glad you're doing something about it."

The angry teen flipped her off as she left, but she didn't see it. Daniel did. "Nicholas, right?"

"Yeah."

"You under eighteen, Nicholas?"

"I'm seventeen."

"You might want to take this opportunity to make a call, before you're officially down to just one. You'll need a parent or guardian to meet you at the station."

He went still. "What do you mean?"

"You're a minor, so you'll have to be released into custody of a parent or guardian."

Nicholas sat up slightly. "But — I don't even live here. I came with friends. My dad's at home, and it's a seven-hour-drive."

Daniel whistled. "You'd better call sooner rather than later, then."

"But — he'll have to take off work!"

"Sorry, son. I was just giving you the heads-up. But you can wait if you want, or let an officer make the call."

He paled. "He's gonna kill me."

"If he does, we'll arrest him. But until he does, you'll need him to get out of holding, so you think about whether you want to call or not."

Nicholas slouched further into the chair, dropping his head, and swore again. After a moment he drew out his phone. "Do I have to do it here?"

Daniel pointed. "There's a corner. We'll try not to eavesdrop."

Nicholas retreated, sitting sideways in the corner and cradling his phone. Daniel turned to Jacob. "So, *Cougars and Cold Ones*."

Jacob's stomach dropped.

"That's the name of the show that's been popping up here. It's all over the con, showing up in video rooms, on panel screens any time there's a gap in the programming. Even had a bunch of old merchandise appear in the dealer room, scattered across booths who didn't recognize it. Somebody seeded it. And man, is that some ugly merch, too. Who ever thought that would sell, even fifteen years ago?"

Jacob risked a breath. "So, you've just been seeing it around?"

"Everyone has. It's all over. Did I miss some internet meme? Is *Cougars and Cold Ones* the new Rick-roll?" He frowned. "Because frankly, I think that's doing Rick Astley a disservice."

Jacob took another breath, more easily now. "Not that I'd heard of. I hope not."

"*Cougars and Cold Ones*?" repeated Paul. "Oh, I remember that! That was years ago, wasn't it?"

"Yeah," agreed a volunteer Jacob didn't recognize. "Some awful reality show about this family from hell. All these dysfunctional crazy people."

"Man, I'd forgotten about that. Yeah, they were nuts."

"I named my dog after that show," said the volunteer. "When we got him, he kept scooting around on the carpet, smearing his butt on everything, so we called him Little Jakey." He laughed. "Turned out he had worms or infected anal glands or something, the vet fixed it. Too bad nobody fixed them. Some people shouldn't breed."

Nicholas' voice rose in the corner. "Dad, I'm sorry! I

didn't — no, I'm sorry! I know you have to work. I know. But the guy says you have to pick me up."

Daniel blew out his breath. "Seven hours. That's not going to be pretty. This will be about the longest seven hours he's ever had to wait."

"Won't be as long as the seven hours home, I'm betting."

"Boom." Daniel gave a jaunty little point in Jacob's direction. "You're right on that one." He glanced at the desk. "What are you working on?"

"Um, just some organizing," he said, his ears growing warm. "Thought I'd get in some practice."

Daniel looked down at the page, eyes running over the mind map and its single dotted line. "Think you're going to solve it before the guys in Homicide?" He softened the joke with a grin.

"That would probably be a ticket straight into the Academy, right?"

"Sure wouldn't hurt anything, I guess."

Jacob swallowed and said casually, "The Academy application — how hard is it?"

"Are you worrying about it? I don't think you have any red flags. Your grades are good, you're taking the right classes, and no issues with the physical, right? Just the psychological profile and background, you should be fine."

"But, the psychological... I mean, that's a pretty big gap, and they can look at anything, and...."

Daniel shrugged. "I guess it does sound kind of scary. But it's not really that bad. They want to be sure that you're coming in for the right reasons, and that there's nothing in your background to make you a risk to yourself or the department."

Jacob looked back at the tablet. "Yeah."

Behind them, Nicholas was off the phone. "He's coming."

"Good," Daniel said.

Nicholas rested his forehead in his hand. "So stupid. No one can afford one of those, they shouldn't cost so much. Stupid."

"Those Hardy Daytonas are really nice," Daniel said. "Very pretty. I'd like one, too, if I had the spare change."

"Shuddup." Nicholas glared at him. "Quit pretending to be a fan. I dunno why you're even dressed up. Cosplay is gay. And you're too old to pretend like you belong at a con."

Daniel crossed his arms and raised an eyebrow. "Son, I was a *Star Wars* fan before you were an itch in your daddy's crotch. If you want something to feel possessive about, go on down to the *My Little Ponies* gathering at the — wait, no, that's a throwback to the eighties show. I guess you'll have to stick with *Doctor Who*. Oops, no, that started in the sixties. Hmm, let's see here." He glanced at the photoshoot gathering schedule on the wall. "Batman and DC villains? Nope. The Marvel Universe? Nope. *Evangelion*? Also before your time."

"Shaddup," growled the kid.

"Ooh, here you go. Your generation has — "

A shriek came from the hall, and Jacob lunged to the door. People were clearing a little space around the girl in the CLUTCH multi-layered garb, who stood frozen, arms half-raised, staring down at herself. Her gorgeous white costume was smeared across the chest and torso with blue-green streaks.

A few feet in front of her, a girl of perhaps fifteen gaped, easing backward. She wore only a narrow plaid tube top and short denim cutoffs over a body covered liberally with grey-green makeup, inexpertly swirled and now smeared in several places. Her multi-colored antennae were crooked.

The spell of shock broke as the scream's echoes faded, and the stained cosplayer's eyes rose from her ruined silks to the grey-green Daisy Duke-like Mole in front of her. Her jaw worked, unable to form words.

"Um — I'm sorry," squeaked the blue-green girl.

"Sorry?" The silken cosplayer looked down at herself again.

The Mole girl bolted. Some of the bystanders shouted after her angrily, but no one stopped her, and she dashed up the escalator, pushing past two more people who recoiled and cried in outrage at fresh grey-green smears, and disappeared down one of the corridors.

Jacob looked back as cosplayers began to gather around the multi-layered silks, two of them carefully folding and protecting her trailing robes as others knelt to look at the makeup stains without touching. "Hydrogen peroxide?" someone asked.

"I've got a bleach pen," called someone from the crowd.

"That'll eat right through the silk," a girl answered. "We need to get it off."

Jacob phoned Sam. "We've got a cosplay emergency," he said. "Who do I call?"

"Fish Face. They've got a whole kit of everything here, since they're doing workshops. What happened?"

"One of the Moles ran right into the CLUTCH costume. Left blue body makeup all over the white."

Sam's horror was palpable even through the phone. "What? Oh, I'll kill him. Unless someone already has."

"Not funny today, Sam. She's by Ops, if you want to come help."

"I'll call Fish Face and meet you there with whatever I can borrow."

A man in an elegant Victorian suit pushed gently through to kneel beside the stricken cosplayer. "Don't rub it, or it'll set worse," he warned. "Is this oil-based?" He scowled at it. "What the heck is this stuff? Anybody have a clue?"

"Some sort of Halloween kit, I'll bet," said someone else. "What a nightmare."

The cosplayer had begun to cry. "We'll never get it out!" She started to rub away tears and then caught herself before she touched her elaborate makeup.

"Excuse me," Jacob said. "I just called someone, and she's coming here with an emergency kit. She might have something to blot it out."

She nodded, sniffing. "I was on my way to judging. Guess there's no point now."

"No, no, you can do it!" said the man in the suit. "Just tell the judges what happened. It's not like nothing like this has ever happened before — though this is pretty bad. But they'll understand. And this is beautiful; it deserves to be judged."

"I'll go and tell them you've been delayed, and why," Jacob offered. "Then it's official and everything. And Sam will be here any minute with Fish Face's kit, and they'll get you taken care of. Okay?"

She sniffed and nodded.

"What's your entry info?"

"I'm FallingStar, entry M-18, dressed as Achenar from *Crooked Running Water* by CLUTCH, the Heavenly Wedding arc, artbook version."

Cosplayers. Couldn't give a simple answer when an enthusiastic one would do. Jacob nodded. "I'll tell them."

Chapter Eighteen

The mobile app guided Jacob to the rear of the hotel's convention center, where he found a couple of groups of people in stunning costumes chatting in the hallway outside a closed room with a sign taped to the door, *Please Knock*.

An assistant sat outside the room with a clipboard, and Jacob approached her. "Your entry M-18 is going to be late. She had an accident coming here."

"Oh, no!"

"She's okay, the costume is not. They're working on it."

The assistant looked down at the board. "She's our last one, but we can wait a bit. You said she's still coming?"

"I think they're going to talk her into it." Sam could be very persuasive, and she'd wanted all day to gush over the costume. The Achenar wouldn't stand a chance.

"Okay, thanks for letting us know."

He nodded toward the closed door. "Can I just talk to them for a second? I told her I'd explain to the judges what happened. It's going to be a little stained."

The assistant's eyes widened. "Oh, no!" She considered. "Normally I'd just have you leave a message with me, but this entry will be done in about thirty seconds —" she indicated the stopwatch feature on her phone and rapped on the door behind her — "and since there's only one entry waiting, you can go in then. Just don't take too long."

"I'll be quick, promise."

She watched the timer count down and then stood to

open the door. Inside, a panel of four costumed judges thanked a fifth person, a young man in a brightly-colored video game costume Jacob couldn't quite place. He left, and Jacob slipped in behind him.

"Well, that one's easy," said one judge, writing a single line and then making an inky slash down the scoresheet.

"His seams were pretty neat," said another. She was dressed as a Twi'lek Jedi. "And I don't think it was all commercial."

"But we don't know that he did any of it," said the first. He was Disney's Aladdin, complete with stuffed monkey on his shoulder. "And he was obviously willing to lie about parts of it. He could have commissioned it all."

The fourth judge, a member of the Bene Gesserit Sisterhood, looked perplexed. "Okay, I obviously missed something."

"You're the needlework expert, so it probably didn't stand out to you. But he said he carved and painted that sword, right?"

"Sure. I've known a lot of people who did their swords."

"Yeah, but theirs probably didn't have a commercial screen-print."

The fourth judge's mouth formed into an outraged little circle. "What? Yeah, I don't do enough with props. Good catch. And wow, what a jerk. Just be honest and it would have been fine, you know? Yeah, even if he did some of it himself, after that, no."

They finished marking their clipboards and one turned to Jacob by the door. "Um, hi. Can we help you?"

"I'm with Con Aid. There was a costume accident, and I promised I'd tell you what happened so you'd understand."

He explained briefly about the Mole and the white silk. "I think they're going to talk her into coming anyway, but she's pretty upset. Obviously."

The judges wore various expressions of dismay. "Man, these kids are out of control," said Aladdin. "If you aren't going to buy proper makeup and learn to use it, don't use it at all!"

"It's mostly the younger ones, at least. They don't know any better." The Twi'lek glanced down at her own body makeup.

"Destroying the hotel and someone else's work is not the way to learn."

"Tell her that of course we won't worry about the makeup stains," said a woman in brassy steampunk. "Just get here whenever she can, and we'll fit her in before the masquerade."

"Thanks, I'll tell her."

"Hey, it just means we get a chance to eat something," said the Bene Gesserit with a grin. "I'm starving. Unless the rumors of no food are true?"

"The hotel restaurants and food court are shut down," Jacob said, "but there are energy bars and microwavable foods and stuff for sale in the lobby."

"Better than nothing," said the Twi'lek. "Are there any good energy bars, or are they all that crumbly granola crap that tastes like cardboard?"

"Granola can be good," said the Bene Gesserit.

"When there's chocolate and fruit on top of it, yeah. Not by itself."

"I'm with her," said Aladdin. "Give me some flavor with my fiber."

"I think there are a variety of brands and flavors," Jacob said with a facetiously placating tone. "So I have to ask, do people freak out, getting judged by a Bene Gesserit?"

She smiled. "Hey, you recognized it! When I was getting breakfast this morning a guy wanted a picture with me and then said he was going to tweet everyone that he'd found Professor McGonagall." She rolled her eyes.

"Let's get some bars, at least, while we wait," said the woman in steampunk. She shifted a tool apron on her hip. "Don't look a gift break in the mouth, yo."

"I'll go get some after this next entry," said the Twi'lek. "Anyone opposed to chocolate and fruit? No?"

"Thanks for telling us about the accident."

Jacob excused himself and left. He hadn't gotten far down the hall when Sergio's voice called to him.

He turned, and Sergio came hurrying toward him, his face strained. "Jacob, man, you've got to help me. You understand this police stuff. They think I did it — someone told them I'd made death threats against the MEGAN!ME executives in my panel yesterday. I said it was a metaphor, an exaggeration, but they think I'm a suspect."

Sergio dropped into one of the lobby couches. "Oh, man, what am I gonna do? Yeah, I said a MEGAN!ME exec should get hit by a bus — but that's not the same thing as killing someone! It's sarcasm, it's exaggeration, it's a lame joke. Probably I shouldn't have said it, I get that. But now I'm a suspect."

"They're not really suspicious, or you wouldn't be having this conversation with me right now," Jacob said, hoping he sounded reassuring. "If they were convinced, or even fairly suspicious, they'd detain you. What'd they say? How did they know?"

"I'm guessing someone told them from the panel yesterday. They knew the topic, knew what I said — knew it better than I did, really. I didn't remember. But good grief, I didn't mean it to sound like some sort of call to rise and murder the evil distribution overlords! It was just a figure of speech."

"They know that," Jacob said. "Again, if they really thought you were the murderer, you'd be at the station right now and waiting to meet your state-appointed lawyer. They're just being thorough." He hoped he was right.

"They told me not to leave without talking to them, even after the con tomorrow."

"That's pretty standard. They have to tell everyone that." That was a bit of a fudge, but Sergio was visibly relaxing, so it was likely worth it.

"You sure? Okay. But — man, it's terrifying, you know?"

Jacob nodded. "Oh yeah. I'm sure it is. I can't imagine."

Sergio blew out his breath. "I was trying to think if there's anything else that would get me in trouble.... I wrote a couple of angry Facebook posts, about *Mr. Doobles* and stuff. Not about illegally downloading or anything, just about MEGAN!ME being a jerk by C-and-D'ing everyone even while not releasing anything from the past decade. Do you think I should take those down? Delete them?"

Jacob shook his head. "I'm pretty sure they can get archives if they want them, and deleting stuff looks more suspicious, I think. If all you said was that the company was jumping on fans and that they haven't released anything, that's true, and you're entitled to your opinion about it. People get mad at companies all the time without going as far as killing anyone."

Sergio nodded. Now he looked almost normal again. "Yeah. Okay. Thanks, man. I didn't mean to freak out, it's just — that was pretty freaky." He looked at the couch. "What's all this blue stuff smeared on here?"

Jacob sighed. "Probably more Mole makeup. Some of the cosplayers used bad makeup and didn't seal themselves, and they're making a mess everywhere. Even trashed a really nice masquerade costume when a girl ran into it."

Sergio's eyebrows rose. "Ouch. Did that end in another murder? Because I know a few people who would call it justifiable."

"Not really funny right now."

"Sorry."

Jacob's phone buzzed with an incoming text. *Where are you? Really need you.*

"Hey, Con Ops needs me. Gotta go. You okay?"

"Yeah, I'm good. Thanks."

Chapter Nineteen

Daniel looked harried and weary, as if his Imperial officer persona had just heard the Emperor was coming to personally supervise the con. "Can you cover the office for a while? I've got to take a statement from the vendor who had the statue stolen, and someone's got to hold the fort here."

"Sure," Jacob said. He dropped into the chair beside the computer. "I can check on what's going with the photo submissions, anyway."

They had several hundred pictures in Flickr, and another hundred or so in the Twitter column. A few were obvious fakes — one of a staged strangulation behind a love seat, and two with llamas edited into the background. What was wrong with people? Humor was one thing, but not during a homicide investigation.

Another fake looked nearly normal but for a Deadpool cosplayer added in the background. Jacob smiled a little at that one. Still unhelpful, but at least thematic.

Mickey came into the conference room. "Hey, is it okay if I just crash in here for a minute? Green room's been turned into a food booth, to try to cut the lines going through the lobby, and the staff suite is like a mobile police station right now."

Jacob gestured to a chair. "Feel free."

"Thanks." Mickey sighed. "Kind of a roller coaster weekend, right?"

"For the con? Yeah, you could say that."

Mickey looked at him. "You're the guy who's doing the police internship or something, right?"

"I'm studying to go into law enforcement, and I'm applying to the Police Academy soon."

"Yeah, that's close enough." Mickey pressed his lips together and seemed to make a decision. "I've got a question for you, then. If something is going to come out, that maybe makes someone look more connected to a murder than he should be — if it's something that he's got good reason to keep hidden, previously — should he bring it up himself or wait until he's asked about it?" One corner of his mouth rose. "I'm asking for a friend."

Jacob gave the joke a half-smile in acknowledgment. "You know, I'm not really qualified to answer for your friend."

"My friend doesn't expect an answer worthy of legal counsel. Just a, you know, suggestion or something. It's a tough call."

"If it's going to come out anyway," Jacob said, "it might be good to bring it up first, explain it if there's a good reason. But you certainly don't have to. Legally, there's no obligation. And if you — your friend does want legal counsel, my aunt's an attorney, and she's here at the con."

"Really?" Mickey brightened, and then he sagged again. "Nah. Attorneys cost money, and you're probably right already." He sighed. "You know how they say that you ask for advice when you already know what you should do and you're just hoping to hear something different? Yeah, that."

Jacob wasn't sure how to respond. "What are you going to tell them?"

"Not that I killed anyone, if that's what you're thinking. Just that there's some stuff that's going to make me look bad."

"Hello?" Detective Martin leaned into the pass-through. "Hey, are there any candy bars or anything in there? The lines are a mile long out here."

"Well, shoot fire and save the matches," Mickey drawled in a ridiculous accent. "Can't argue with that kind of timing. You got a minute, officer?"

She raised an eyebrow. "Detective, and yes, but I'm fresh out of matches."

"I was just wondering if I should tell you something, and here you are. Can I give you some info?"

She raised a finger, and then she left the pass-through and came through the door, closing it behind her. "Always available to hear something helpful, Mr. — Groene?"

"Yes, Mickey Groene." He pulled a chair nearer.

Jacob fished under the table and found a couple of candy bars. Vince hadn't sent everything to the vending tables. He tossed one to each of them.

"This has to be on the record, Mr. Groene."

"Oh, I know. That's why I'm talking to you. I figure it's better if you hear it from me."

Detective Martin nodded toward Jacob. "Would you like to go somewhere else to talk?"

"Thanks, but I don't know how much it's going to matter now that she's dead." He took a breath. "I'm connected to Valerie Kimberton, but nobody knows it. I didn't kill her, but you always hear that police look for family and friends first."

"And which are you?"

"I'm dating her sister."

Sister. Jacob thought for a moment. Yes, Christopher had mentioned a sister, an artist who would design the *chibi* mascot to replace him.

Detective Martin nodded. "And why is this a secret?"

"Valerie and I work in the same industry, not exactly together but in the same circles. I'm a voice actor, she's an executive in a dubbing and distribution company. I do some voice work for MEGAN!ME, and it could get uncomfortable if people think I'm getting hired for some other reason than my professional talent."

"Right." Detective Martin stopped and looked at Mickey. "What did you think of Valerie?"

"Will Sophie ever hear this?"

"Not unless it's introduced as evidence."

"And if that happens, we're probably already done, anyway." Mickey sighed. "I'm going to be honest with you, Valerie was a fairly terrible person to be around. If someone really did kill her, it was an extreme and horrible action — but it probably wasn't a random act of violence."

"Why do you say that?"

"You want specific examples?" Mickey shook his head. "I could give you some, but I'm betting you're already hearing stories as you're talking to people. Let's just say that Valerie wasn't afraid to throw her weight around. I hear a rumor she was making life miserable even here at the con for Vince, since MEGAN!ME was a big sponsor. She probably thought that gave her the right to be queen or something."

"What did you hear about Vince and Valerie?"

Mickey spread his hands, gesturing vaguely. "I didn't see anything specific myself, if that's what you mean. More of a general vibe among everyone."

"I saw them, yesterday afternoon, in the dealer hall," offered Jacob. "She was yelling at him because there was a typo in the program guide, using an I instead of an exclamation mark. Dressing him down right in front of the whole con. She wanted him to recall all the program guides and reprint them — which is impossible, because the program guides were already being distributed and because you can't just get a run of eight thousand books done as a walk-in while-you-wait sort of thing. Not to mention the cost."

Mickey was nodding. "Typical. Not that she necessarily cared about the typo that much, but it gave her leverage for something else."

"Like?" Detective Martin looked between them.

Jacob shrugged. "I heard her say she'd pull her sponsorship if it wasn't fixed, but I don't know if that was what she wanted to do or just another threat."

"Yeah." Mickey sighed. "That was Valerie. I don't know if she could have, but she would have threatened to."

Detective Martin was making notes. "Was that significant to Vince? What would happen if she did?"

Now Mickey shrugged. "Running conventions is not my gig. I don't know how Con Job is doing, none of my business."

"Vince said it was tight this year," Jacob recalled. "That's why Reg is being done in house with spreadsheets, instead of using one of the event services."

"Reg?"

"Registration. Everything's done by hand in spreadsheets, which is slow and makes for mistakes." He held up his badge. "I wasn't supposed to have my real full name as my badge name, but that's what happens when someone enters the data wrong."

Detective Martin nodded. "Is that typical, do you know? Not the badges, but being tight on funds?"

"This isn't Comic Con San Diego," Mickey said. "It's not a Hollywood love fest. Most of these smaller and mid-size cons are a labor of love, just funding themselves. All the people you're seeing work Registration, checking badges, even selling the energy bars out there are volunteers, not staff. And the staff at these smaller cons get paid in hotel rooms and food for the weekend. Nobody's making money off this."

"Going back to what you wanted to tell me," Detective Martin said, "how did you meet this — Sophie?"

"Yeah, Sophie. I met her at a bookstore, actually, about two years ago. It was in Delaware, I had a little time to kill after a con, so I went to find something to read on the plane. She was browsing in Historicals, she recommended a couple of titles, and in the end we got some coffee at the bookstore."

"And you didn't know who she was."

"No way. Kimberton isn't such a unique name, and I — I told her I was in video games at first, which was sort of true. I do a lot of game voices. But you don't tend to tell people right away, or they just want to hear voices all the time. I told her later, of course, and that's when it started to come out, when she was all, Oh, my sister's company does a lot of voice dubbing."

"And did you tell Valerie?"

"I think Sophie did. She'd already mentioned me to her family, and she didn't realize that Valerie and I had already worked together. Valerie — she didn't exactly hold it over my head, that would be unfair to say. We had a kind of unspoken agreement not to talk about it, as it wouldn't have done either of us any good."

Detective Martin nodded. "Had she ever threatened you with this?"

"What? No, no, nothing like that. Like I said, she couldn't bring it out without hurting both of us. It was kind of a nuclear deterrent. There was no advantage in it for her."

"So you had nothing against her?"

"Well, this is probably stupid to say while her murder's

being investigated, but I can't honestly say that. She wasn't a nice person. I'd rather stick a fork in my ear than spend another Thanksgiving with her. But it's a lot easier for me to just skip Thanksgiving than to kill her — and at a con, full of my colleagues and fans. This would just be stupid."

"I agree," said Detective Martin, "but murder is pretty much always stupid, and that doesn't stop a lot of people." She closed her notebook. "Still, this kind of honesty doesn't exactly rocket you to suspect number one. Thanks for telling me about it."

"Thanks." He hesitated. "Um, you'd tell me if I should be worried, right? Like, if that's enough to get me on a suspect list?"

Detective Martin smiled. "Mr. Groene, right now we have a suspect list of about eight thousand people, which is to say we have a suspect list of none. I don't think your love life is likely to put you in danger, but if that changes, I'll break the news as early and gently as I can."

"You're a good cop," he said. "Here, lemme buy you another." He pushed the untouched candy bar over to her.

"Thanks, but I'm on duty." She grinned. "What about Valerie's family? How's her relationship with her parents, any other siblings?"

"Her family's not so bad, I don't think. No money issues that I know of, either. I mean, they all know she flies on a broomstick, but she's been like that forever and they just live with it. They weren't even really surprised when—" He stopped. "Oh, why didn't I think of this? Valerie got a death threat."

Detective Martin straightened. "What?"

"She told everyone about it last Thanksgiving. She was kind of proud of it — which might have been a front, and maybe she was scared, but all she was saying was that it showed how much she was shaking things up in the industry."

"Who from?"

"Some fan," Mickey said. "Someone mad about MEGAN!ME's handling of its catalog."

Jacob's stomach tightened. Not Sergio. Sergio wouldn't have done anything so stupid, surely....

"Do you have a name?" She flipped back a few pages in her notebook, and Jacob was sure she was thinking of Sergio. "Did she tell you who it was?"

But Mickey shook his head. "It was just a kid, I think. She showed us the email, and it looked like a third grader had written it — which I guess is like a high-schooler nowadays, but still. He was just mad, it was obvious."

"But someone's killed her."

"Even given the fact that he couldn't punctuate, capitalize, or spell, he'd have to be a pretty dim bulb to think that killing Valerie would get *Mr. Doobles* out of the vault."

"What's *Mr. Doobles*? Is it valuable?"

"To the fans, maybe," Jacob offered. "It's a show, about a bunch of kids who draw stories. Huge fanbase, cute show. It's been running about fifteen years, but MEGAN!ME has the US license, and they haven't released any new episodes for over a decade."

"Why not?"

Mickey lifted a shoulder. "Who can say? But MEGAN!ME sends a cease-and-desist to everyone who scans or rips or previews anything from an overseas release. Which is illegal, sure, but which obviously angers the fans because they can't legally get anything from the last ten years."

"Why don't they just order it from overseas? Or do they need the voices dubbed?"

Mickey shook his head. "*Mr. Doobles* fans don't need the dub. Hey, I make a good chunk of my living doing dubs, and I'll admit upfront that most fans prefer *Mr. Doobles* straight and wouldn't even blink if they just had subtitles. But MEGAN!ME holds the US license, which means it's illegal for anyone in the US to order it from anywhere else. If they order a DVD from, say, a UK company, they're breaking international copyright law."

Detective Martin blinked. "That's silly, if it's not available to buy here."

"Don't expect anyone to line up to argue. Even the creators are getting screwed, since no one can buy any *Mr. Doobles* material except for second-hand copies originally put out by Pop Culture, which of course pays no royalties."

"But can't they sue MEGAN!ME then, for failing to distribute?"

"Nope. It's a license, not a distribution contract. An option, not an obligation. If they decide they don't want to mess with a title, or if they pick it up in a bundle with something else, they don't have to do a thing with it. But then no one else can buy or sell it."

Detective Martin's eyebrows drew together. "So what are the fans supposed to do?"

"Get mad or break the law. Or both. It's harder to import a DVD, since a lot of companies can't or won't ship licensed titles to the US, plus the whole region mess, so they can't buy them legally from out of the country. So, piracy."

"Well." Detective Martin looked faintly offended. "I didn't know it could work like that."

"Yep. And off the record, it's hard to blame them when there's a MEGAN!ME sitting on titles and making it impossible to do the right thing." He shrugged. "But that's not exactly your murder crowd, you know? They may get upset and vocal, but what it boils down to is, people are mad because they can't pay for a product instead of stealing it."

Detective Martin chuckled. "Okay, I see your point. But you said she did get a death threat."

"She did. And I suppose there could well be some nutcase who thinks killing a VP will release his favorite show because that's what all the voices tell him, but my money's that it was some angry brat who never learned how to talk like a grown-up."

"We probably ought to have the details, just in case."

"I'll bet it's still in her email, saved somewhere. Not because she was worried about it, but because she was proud."

"Proud."

"Proud that she'd managed to make a kid swear at her in bad spelling. That was Valerie, sad as it is to say it." He gave Detective Martin a pleading look. "Don't tell Sophie. She wasn't under any illusions about her sister, but she wouldn't like to hear it said aloud to strangers."

"I wouldn't say anything. Does she know, about her sister?"

"I called her today. I got through a few minutes after her mother did, so she already knew. Still, pretty rough."

Daniel walked in and stopped to look at them. "Am I interrupting something?"

"No," Mickey said. "Except — yes." He ran both hands through his hair. "There's one other thing I should tell you, before you find out from someone else."

Detective Martin flipped her notebook open again. "Yes?"

"I — I need work. Pretty bad. I have a good reputation, some fans, steady roles, but — I could really use the money, you know? Got in a bit deep last year. And… Sorry, all that is just to say that I can't afford to lose any work right now. And Valerie was going to cut me from *Caesar's Ghost*."

"What's that?"

"She told me she was going to pull some strings and drop me. Or, it's a first-person shooter set in ancient Rome, depending on what you're asking."

"Why was she going to do that?"

Mickey sighed. "Because Sophie booked a Caribbean cruise and invited their mom and step-dad, but not Valerie. So she was going to drop me to get back at Sophie." He looked at them. "But I didn't kill her, I swear. I wouldn't do that — especially not to Sophie. But it's going to look bad if it comes out."

Detective Martin exhaled slowly. "Yeah," she said. "It will."

Chapter Twenty

"Well, that was unexpected," Daniel said.

They were in the staff suite, or what had been the staff suite. Now it was full of uniformed and plainclothes police and a single table of candy bars, packaged chips, energy bars, bottled water, cans of soft drinks, and snack-sized packs of trail mix.

Detective Martin propped her feet on an empty chair and popped the top of a can. "Yeah. But he had something about bringing it up before it came up, because I'm finding it a little harder to be suspicious of him. He seemed like a pretty nice guy."

"A lot of them do."

"Yeah, but he's not at the top of my list. That's Vince Corleone."

Daniel raised an eyebrow. "Oh? Why's that?"

"I know he's your convention buddy, but how much do you know about his financial situation?"

"It's not the kind of thing that comes up during Marvel versus DC debates."

"Everyone's got hints that the convention's underwater. Even Jacob here mentioned it." She looked at him. "Come on, I know you're listening."

"Am not," Jacob called. "I didn't hear a thing about Marvel or DC."

"It's okay, I think we can use you." She beckoned him over. "You're not police, you're part of the con. You're our mole."

He gave her a dubious look. "I'm a painted blue-green alien with antennae?"

"I'm betting that's another in-joke," she said wearily, and she took a drink.

"Why Vince?" prompted Daniel.

"The con's in trouble," she resumed, "and people seem surprised by that. Apparently it wasn't struggling the last year or two, and my casual interest with some people has indicated that a convention of this size should be pretty stable and self-sufficient after several years. And Fibbins—" she nodded toward a man in a loose-fitting suit across the room — "says he can smell an embezzler from twenty paces but picked up Vince Corleone at twenty-five."

Daniel gave her an even look. "You talk like old film noir."

"Busted. But it's true, anyway. Fibbins is already talking about going over the accounts with Vince, with the excuse of understanding the MEGAN!ME sponsorship."

Daniel exhaled. "I hope that doesn't turn out to be true."

Detective Martin's face softened. "I hope so too, Daniel, for your sake."

"But that doesn't say anything about the other girl, Trish Kur...."

"Tasha Kurlansky," supplied Detective Martin. "I know. Killing her wouldn't affect the con's finances, or Micky Groene's job, or even that guy who was replaced by the stuffed animal."

"Potential stuffed animal," Daniel corrected. "That was only a rumor."

"Right. Killing Tasha doesn't save him from losing to a

potential stuffed animal. But it can't be a coincidence, not with two killings in two days on the same site with the same method."

"Maybe the first one was a practice murder?" Jacob asked.

"It'd be a stupid practice run," Detective Martin said. "If Valerie was the target, and he killed Tasha for practice, all he did was put us on alert about Valerie's death that much faster."

Jacob's phone buzzed. *Are you busy?* Lydia asked.

He rolled his eyes. *It's been that kind of a day,* he texted back. *What do you need?*

I want to put my new figurine in your room so I don't have to carry it everywhere.

Come by Ops and I'll give you my key.

Busy, can't come at the moment. Can you swing by Gaming?

Jacob chuckled aloud, and Daniel gave him a curious glance. "My aunt," Jacob said. "She's not fooling anyone, she's having as much fun here as any other attendee. You need anything done toward Gaming? I'm headed that way to drop off a room key."

"Play a round of DDR for me," Daniel said.

"Hey, Jacob."

"Sergio! Walk with me. I'm headed to Gaming." He glanced at his friend. "Man, you look kind of green. And it's a bit early for what that cup smells like. You okay? Something else happen about being a suspect?"

Sergio's mouth twitched. "I just found out I'm about seven thousand dollars in the hole."

"What? What happened?"

"You know Rick Yoshinaga?"

"Name is vaguely familiar, but no."

"He's a photographer."

"Oh, yeah, got it. What about him?"

The Gaming room was a long room, subdivided from a larger ballroom. One end was full of arcade machines, consoles, and musical games such as Guitar Hero, DDR, and Rock Band. The other had a mosaic of tables at which groups of various sizes leaned over card games, board games, dice games, and arrays of small figures on maps.

"He wanted to get into videography," said Sergio, "start a company. Do weddings, cons, graduations, promo films, small projects and stuff." The tall Starbucks cup wasn't full of coffee, and it probably wasn't Sergio's first. He was going to talk a lot. "But that's an expensive business to get into. Lots of equipment."

"I'm guessing about seven thousand dollars' worth?"

"He'd been talking about it for a while, and then last year at Con-nundrum we were drinking in his room, and he told me he was ready to get started, that he even had the ideal project coming up and he was pretty sure he could land it if he just had the equipment."

"Is this where I ask how much you'd been drinking?"

Lydia was at a far table, her tablet propped up in front of her. Jacob started in that direction.

"I've known Yoshinaga a long time. I thought he was a good guy. And I kind of still think he is — I know, just wait for it. And we'd had two bottles of Jack by then. Anyway, my grandma had just died and left me some cash, and I agreed to front him seven grand, and he would pay me back with a thousand extra after the big deal. That's good investment."

"Fast forward to the payoff?"

"Supposed to be this month. But I just talked to Yoshinaga, and he says.... He says he sank all my money and all his money into equipment. Got a small biz loan, bought a ton of stuff. He said he landed the project, got the deposit, and was supposed to get paid the balance last month."

"What happened?"

"The project lost funding. Went bankrupt, I guess. But he'd only gotten a deposit upfront, not anything close to the quote he'd turned in. Which was supposed to pay for all the equipment he'd borrowed money to get. And now they're not paying him."

"So he can't pay you."

"So he can't pay me, and he's in debt for the stuff he bought, and we're both burned. And even if I sue him — which I probably could, we wrote a sort of agreement that night — I can't get blood from a turnip, and he's dead broke now. And it's not his fault the company went bankrupt or whatever."

"Can't he sue them for his payment?"

Sergio shook his head. "I think that's what bankrupt means, right? That they don't have to pay what they owe? My uncle got burned by that a couple of times. Did work for companies that knew they were going to file, and so they never had to pay him. It's a real jerk maneuver."

"Look, why don't you ask Lydia about it tomorrow?" suggested Jacob. "It's not her field, but she can at least tell you if there's anything worth pursuing. And if she doesn't know, she can point you toward someone else."

"Good idea," said Sergio. "I'll do that." He shook his head. "I just hope...."

"What?" Jacob looked at him. "Oh, no. What?"

"I thought I was getting eight thousand dollars this month!" Sergio said defensively. "I put stuff on the credit card, figuring I'd have the money to pay it off when it came due."

Jacob fought the urge to plant his face in his palm. "Don't spend money you don't have," he muttered. "Ever."

"What?"

"Trust me on this. You spend money you don't have, you get in debt, you'll do anything to get out of it. Sell anything, even your soul. Even other people's souls. And you can't change it afterward, and it'll follow you forever."

Now Sergio looked worried for him. "You okay? You're talking like some sort of remorseful hit man."

Jacob snorted. "I'm just getting into character to drop in at an RPG table. Bah, I was young, I needed the gold pieces." He looked at Sergio. "Talk to Lydia tomorrow. And talk to your credit card company, see if you can work something out before they slap you with a zillion percent interest."

He left Sergio and crossed to Lydia's table. There were six around the table, all with folded name cards sitting in front of them. Lydia's read *Hotspur le PewPew.*

She didn't see him coming, as she looked from the grid to the character sheet on her tablet. "I've already cast Aspect of the Falcon, so now I'm targeting the druid." She rolled dice. "Natural twenty! With my competence bonus, that's a thirty-two, with a potential critical."

"Roll to confirm."

She dropped a die and pumped her fist. "Yes! Crit hit. That's—" she rolled a handful of dice — "fifty-three points of damage. Boo-yeah!"

The game-master rolled a die behind his cardstock

shield and made a face. "Well, that pretty much wrecked his day. The druid face-plants hard. He drops the crystalline ball, and it's rolling across the floor, toward the east." He set a small marker on the room map. "Next turn, Gunthor."

A man sat forward, hand on his chin. "Well, I was going to rage, but there's kind of no target left. So I guess I'd better get the crystal thing." He deepened his voice and rumbled, "Gunthor grab!"

"And now we're out of combat, so I'm going to say even though it's rolling pretty briskly, you can snatch it without much trouble. So now you've got the final piece of the puzzle."

"We'd better stabilize the druid," said another man in the requisite black t-shirt. His read, *Can't sleep, Con will eat me.* "We need to keep him around to question."

"Hey," Jacob said, squatting beside his aunt's chair. "What's up?"

"Oh, hi," said Lydia. "We're busy solving a murder. Kind of like if *Clue* were done by an insane wizard."

"Good luck with that," he said. He dropped a key card on the table beside her dice. "Room four one six. What'd you get?"

Lydia gestured toward an over-sized bag on the floor beneath her chair, still following the game, and Jacob bent to look into it. It was the splendid Cloud Strife and Hardy Daytona figure. "Oh. A kid got arrested today for trying to steal that, you know."

Lydia raised an eyebrow. "Does he need counsel? His fee should about cover the cost."

"You're cold, you know that?"

Lydia hummed the bass line shared by "Under Pressure" and "Ice, Ice Baby."

The GM rolled a die and chuckled. "Oh, boy. Okay, so

the crystalline ball is still in the barbarian's hands. It quivers and then breaks open, and a puddle of ink spills out onto the floor, forming the final letter. You can now attempt to solve the second riddle of the captain's death."

The barbarian's player looked about the table. "And the rest of my party is still looking at that book across the room."

"That's right."

The player grinned. "Gunthor hero! They not invite Gunthor to special book just because Gunthor can't read. But Gunthor prove wrong!"

Around the table, the group began to groan in anticipation. A woman put her hand over her eyes. "Absolutely nothing can go wrong here."

"Okay, you've got all the letters, and you just have to unscramble them to learn the murder weapon." The GM looked at Gunthor's player, grinning. "Roll a D-twenty and add your Intelligence modifier."

The player spun a die and snorted a laugh. "Well," he announced gleefully, "that's a one, minus two, for a negative one."

The GM took a breath and managed to suppress most of his laughter. "You look at the collected letters and unscramble them. You are shocked — shocked! — to discover that Venture Captain Barillo was killed with a gnu!"

Shrieks of laughter rose from the group.

"I'm heading back now," said Jacob. "Don't leave tonight with the key, okay?"

"Are you kidding?" Lydia answered. "The way this con is going? I'm not going anywhere."

Chapter Twenty One

"Hey, Jacob."

He looked up to see Jessica and vibrant-haired Amber leaning over the pass-through. "Hey, guys. What's up?"

"I brought Amber to answer your questions."

"What questions?"

"About arsenate pesticides." Amber tucked pink and purple hair behind her ear and adjusted the ear cuff. "I'm an advocate with Consumer Actions."

"Really? I never knew that's what you did." Jacob checked his phone to verify the substance name. "So, lead hydrogen arsenate. Sound familiar?"

"Lead and arsenic were really common as pesticides," said Amber. "In the early 1900s people were actually getting sick from fruit treated with lead arsenate pesticides, and some boards of health were actually rejecting or destroying crops because they considered them dangerous. And this is like only fifteen or twenty years after *The Jungle*, you know? It's still a big deal that they're even acting on this."

"So they banned it?"

"Oh, no way. They were using that stuff on fruit tree bugs and crabgrass and mosquitoes. Kills everything, you know, so we weren't going to give it up just because it could kill us too. Lead arsenate wasn't banned until the eighties, and there's still some arsenic herbicides out there now. Heck, we can feed it to our livestock."

"What?"

"Yep, there's three or four arsenic compounds that are used to bulk up chickens and pigs for market. There's a lot of talk about it in the industry, because the arsenic shows up in the chicken meat, and some of it has been pulled by the manufacturers at least temporarily. But the FDA hasn't withdrawn its approval yet, so it's all still legal and stuff."

"Ew," said Sam. "Are you serious?"

Amber twisted her mouth. "Why do you think I eat organic?"

"Makes sense, if it's arsenic-free."

"Well, no arsenic can be used in organic production, so it's a lot safer, but it's not foolproof. A lot of lead arsenate is left in the soil, and so it still shows up in crops. Rice is a big one for that. I've read estimates of two hundred pounds of arsenic were applied per acre, over the years. Think about that." She shuddered. "About ten or fifteen years ago, the EPA pulled a bunch of topsoil out of people's yards in a subdivision built in a former orchard. The lead and arsenic were causing birth defects in their kids."

Sam swore. "That's crazy. And why isn't anyone talking about this? Seems like arsenic in the chicken would be big news."

Amber shook her head. "There's a few warnings about things like mushroom collecting and stuff — morels pick up a lot of lead and arsenic from treated soil and can be dangerous — but what's the point of scaring people when there's nothing they can do about it? So your backyard dirt might be causing birth defects or learning disorders, or your *arroz con pollo* might be carcinogenic, but what are they going to do?" She shrugged. "We're pushing for changes in current production, which is hard enough, but things like arsenic in the soil, that's hard to deal with."

"So, you can still buy this stuff?"

"Sort of. Like I said, some of the animal feed stuff has been voluntarily suspended, but it could come back, and in the meantime it's not illegal to buy or sell or use whatever's already out there. Same with the herbicides, and you can buy some of those right in your local home improvement store. Plus, you could mix up your own lead arsenate at home, or at least a lot of the old farmers used to do that."

"Ah," said Jacob flatly. "So you don't have to get it from China."

"Oh, no," Amber said easily. "No, there's a fair bit of talk about arsenic in Chinese produce — and it's not really without cause, because for all that they're not supposed to be using it, lots of import crops test positive for it. But it's certainly not limited to China."

"Well," said Jacob, with a guilty ripple of relief, "there goes that theory."

"What's that?"

"I'd thought — I'd wondered, if lead arsenate was being used in China but not here, that maybe the person who was using it had gotten it from China. But that's not going to be very compelling, if I could just go down to Lowe's and buy this stuff."

"What you buy at Lowe's or Home Depot is a little different," Amber clarified, "but yeah, it certainly didn't have to come from China."

"You're saying it could have come from just about anywhere."

"Anyone with access to old farm supplies could have it, or access to a garden store, or a basic competency with Google, yeah."

"Thanks." Jacob sighed. "That doesn't exactly narrow our field."

"Hey, guy."

This time it was Ryan Brazil leaning over the pass-through. "I'm Jacob. Can I help you?"

"Yeah. Hey, the green room got stripped and the con suite is full of police and suspects or something. What am I supposed to be doing about coffee?"

It took Jacob a minute to understand the problem. "You want…. There's probably a coffee maker in your room, if it's like mine. And it should be safe, because all the coffee stuff is prepackaged and the water should be fine."

Ryan rolled his eyes. "I'm not drinking generic hotel coffee. Who knows where that's been, when it was ground, whatever? I need some Starbucks. Can you call me a volunteer, send them for something before my next panel?"

Jacob blinked at him. "We're running at least four tables of snacks and microwave meals for thousands of attendees. We're all having a little make-do. I don't think there's going to be a volunteer available."

Ryan swore. "It's like you don't even *want* guests here." He blew out his breath in noisy exasperation. "Can you at least get me some bottled water or something?"

Getting Ryan what he wanted would get him out of everyone's hair for a while. Yes, it would further his spoiled attitude, but maybe his next entitlement tantrum wouldn't be Jacob's problem. "Sure. But I'll have to go get something from one of the stations. Tell you what, you wait in the conservatory, and I'll bring it out."

He left Con Ops and went to the former staff suite. He

slid up the side of the long line and went around the back of the table. "Hi," he said, showing his Con Aid badge. "I need a bottle of water for a guest."

"Is it Ryan Brazil?" asked the girl, pulling more macaroni and cheese from the cardboard case.

"Uh, yeah."

"Of course it is." She passed Jacob a bottle of water. "Last one for being a guest. Next one he has to pay for. We've got a lot of people to take care of here."

"Right. I'll tell him."

Jacob took the bottle out to the conservatory. Several fandom groups were still photographing their gatherings, and he could see a group of several Battletech Houses and mercenary companies, a collection of Buffy characters, three Sherlocks in iconic hat and scarf, and an assortment of Alices from various Wonderland incarnations. He'd missed the costume contest, and he wondered how his friends had fared.

Ryan Brazil was on a couch, staring at his tablet. He was facing away, and as Jacob drew near he could see that Ryan was flipping through a photo album, dwelling on some and skipping over others. "Here's your water."

"Oh!" Ryan pulled the tablet to his chest and reached for the bottle. "Thanks. I'd wondered what happened to you."

"Had to go pick it up," Jacob answered. "They say that's your last free one, sorry. They've got a lot of demand and they need to save some for the attendees."

"Are you kidding me? The attendees don't make a living off their voices, you know."

"I'm just the messenger." Jacob glanced down at the tablet Ryan held near him, hovering as if he were undecided whether to conceal it or leave it on his lap where Jacob might be able to see it.

Nothing is so intriguing as what someone wishes to

hide. "Catching up on Facebook?" Jacob asked.

"Yeah."

"Who's that?"

Ryan hesitated only a second or so. "You think she's cute? She is, but don't get any ideas. She's my niece." He lowered the tablet and displayed a photo of a girl in her mid-teens, smiling at the camera with one hand on her popped hip. Jacob thought she was dressed as a Pokemon character.

"Cute," Jacob agreed, "but a bit young for me."

"Yep," Ryan said. "Don't want any pervs or creepers." He brushed the screen as he reached for the power button, flipping to the next photo as the tablet screen went dark.

"Wait," said Jacob. "Who was that?"

"Oh, that's her sister," Ryan said. "She's older, but still, no ideas."

"Can I at least see her?"

Ryan hesitated. "That's kind of not cool."

"Oh, come on. I don't even know your niece."

Ryan shook his head. "Nope, sorry."

Jacob swallowed. "Okay. You've got a panel coming up, right? Hope it goes well."

He headed back to Con Ops, his mind racing. It had gone by too quickly to be sure — but he thought that second photo had been Sam.

But Sam wasn't Ryan Brazil's niece, so it couldn't have been her. But he was pretty sure he'd seen that photo before. It had been a cosplay photo, a white gown before a stand of trees, and not too many people had done the School Days arc of *Season of the Dove*. While it was plausible that Ryan Brazil's nieces were fans, it seemed less likely that one would do the identical costume in the identical setting as Sam.

Jacob went directly to the computer at Con Ops and

opened Facebook. Sam usually had a couple of albums documenting her latest costumes. He opened the first and stopped.

That was the photo — the exact photo. He was certain of it. Sam had been on Ryan Brazil's tablet, and her profile was closed to non-friends.

Which wouldn't be that weird, because Sam was pursuing voice acting and might be networking, except that Ryan had called her his niece and had tried to conceal the tablet.

He texted Sam. *You busy?*

Helping someone with zombie makeup for tonight, nearly done. What's up?

It was an awkward question to ask via text. He decided not to. *Can you come by Ops when you're done?*

Chapter Twenty Two

Jacob couldn't see what was being submitted to the Flickr account, as it was administrated by the police. But photos shared via the Twitter hashtag were open to all, and he scrolled slowly down them. What was it the thief had wanted to hide? Was it related to either of the murders?

"Freaking idiots."

Jacob turned as Daniel came in. The Imperial uniform was starting to look rumpled. "What happened?"

"The whole dance just got Rick-rolled, only instead of Rick Astley it was that *Cougars and Cold Ones* show again. What the heck? What is this thing?"

Ice settled into Jacob's stomach. This was no coincidence.

"Where is it coming from, and why here? People are starting to make jokes about it, which is fine except—"

"Daniel."

Daniel stopped and looked at him. "What is it?"

Jacob took a breath. "It's...."

"What? You're not doing this. Putting these videos—"

"No! No, I'm not doing it. I would never. But...."

Daniel sat down and leaned back, deliberately casual. "I'm listening."

Jacob exhaled and shook his head. "Nothing."

"Fine. I sometimes forget what I'm going to say, too." Daniel gave him a sidelong look.

Jacob was saved by Detective Martin's entrance. She

was clutching a tall paper cup of coffee. "This stuff is getting rare. The barristas say they've been hammered this afternoon."

Sam leaned over the pass-through. "Hey, Jacob, what'd you need?"

"Come on in here." He turned and looked at the police officers. "And I'm glad you guys are here, too. 'Cuz this is kind of weird."

Sam came in and gave him an odd look. "What's up?"

"Do you know Ryan Brazil?"

"Of course. Voice actor. Judged the voice contest today, and actually complimented me afterward."

"He did?"

"You don't have to sound surprised," she told him. "He said he wanted to pick me to win but was outvoted, but he thought he could talk me up to some casting people and directors and maybe get my name in. Which I thought was pretty cool of him." She stopped. "Why are you looking at me like that?"

"Did you give him your contact info?"

"Of course. How else could we do business-type talk?"

"So you had a business card or something?"

"No, we friended each other."

"On Facebook."

"That's how some people do business. Less formal, more friendly."

Jacob bit at his lip. "Okay, here's where it gets weird." He paused, trying to put his unease into words, and the silence stretched.

Detective Martin cleared her throat. "If it helps," she said, "I spent two years going after human traffickers before I got into Homicide, so whatever you're going to say isn't going to sound stupid to me."

That lent a more sinister tone to what Jacob had to ask. "Ryan was looking at photos when I took him a bottle of water," he said, "and he kind of tried to hide the pictures from me. They were just photos, nothing porno, but he was kind of, I dunno, weird about them. I asked, and he told me they were of his nieces."

Sam's eyes had changed, but she spoke as if she didn't understand. "Maybe they were."

Jacob tapped the touchpad and the screen flickered to life, showing her in the white gown before the trees. "This photo. He called you his niece and said I couldn't look at your picture."

Sam started to speak and then stopped.

Detective Martin looked at Sam. "How old are you?"

"Twenty-two."

"Not illegal, then, just creepy."

"Not the other girl I saw," Jacob said. "She was maybe fifteen, I'd guess. He even said she was younger, said I shouldn't get any ideas about her."

"And that's both creepy and a potential legal issue," Detective Martin returned. "Not a lot to work on, but that's a definite blip on my admittedly-sensitized radar."

"Can I unfriend him right now or will that blow any potential investigation?" Sam asked, taking out her phone. "Because I've got beach pictures on there, too. And, ew."

"I hear you, but first let's find out what we're dealing with," Detective Martin said. "Who else was at this contest he judged today?"

"Oh, a lot of people. There's a potential voice role at the end of it, so lots of hopefuls like me were there. Ryan judged, so did Mickey Groene and Sandra Shark."

"Oh, I remember Mickey Groene. Let's ask him how it

went today. Any other females about your age?"

"Definitely, but I couldn't tell you who."

Jacob checked the schedule. "Mickey's free right now. Should I try to get him here?"

"No hurry, but sure."

Daniel hadn't spoken yet, but his posture had shifted slightly. Jacob had the impression that didn't bode well for Ryan Brazil.

Jacob turned on the radio. "If anyone sees Mickey Groene, please send him to Con Ops. Alternately, if Guest Relations could give me a way to contact him, we'd appreciate it."

Sam dropped into a chair. "So basically, he lied to me about my voice acting so he could ogle my photos. I don't even know which one I'm more upset about right now."

"Why choose?" Detective Martin asked.

The radio came to life. "I've got Mickey Groene over here at Main. He says he's happy to come by, heading that way now."

Mickey had clearly expected something else. "About the voice acting contest?" he repeated, perplexed.

"Yes. Did anything stand out to you?"

"Well, a few things." He pointed at Sam. "Her, for one thing. She did a great job."

Sam smiled. "Thanks."

Detective Martin frowned. "You and Ryan Brazil, both?"

"Hm? Well, I guess so. He said she was good, too, but

he liked the guy with the goat impression more. It was really down to three people, and — plug your ears and hum, Sam, you're not supposed to hear this — and Sandra and I were pulling for the first guy up and Sam here, but Ryan pushed really hard for the goat-guy and swung the other two."

"Ryan voted against her?" Detective Martin repeated.

Sam's eyes were wide, her expression growing in slow outrage.

"Yeah. Don't take it personally. It's a tough call, and that's why there are multiple judges."

"Oh, it's personal," Sam said, "but not because he didn't like my lines."

Mickey looked from her to the police officers. "I feel like I'm missing something here."

"Mr. Groene, you've been very helpful," Detective Martin said. "Thank you very much for your time. Can we count on you to keep this conversation private for the time being?"

"Certainly. I don't even know what we talked about."

When he had gone, Detective Martin and Daniel exchanged glances. "How do you want to play this?" she asked.

Daniel frowned for a long moment. Finally he interlaced his fingers and stretched, so that a couple of knuckles popped. "None of that was illegal," he said, with obvious reluctance. "Just sleazy."

"Would it be more than sleazy if he's friending minors?" asked Sam.

"Depends on what he's doing once he's friended them." Detective Martin frowned. "And that's where the computer guys have to get involved, see if he's just looking at pics or soliciting pics or what."

"Sam, don't hold your breath waiting for a call from a

director based on Brazil's recommendation," Daniel said. "I'm sorry. But you can maybe take some comfort in the fact that we're going to make his life really uncomfortable if he so much as sticks a toe across the legal line."

"He deliberately sunk me so he could get photos," Sam said. "Holy — I just — there aren't even words." She shook her head. "I'm so un-friending him."

A chorus of shrieks and shrieking laughter drew their attention, and Detective Martin rose and started toward the door. Before she could reach it, however, Zach appeared at the pass-through. "Hey, guys!" He beckoned them with a wave of his arm. "Have you seen this? The zombie crawl is starting, and it's awesome."

Chapter Twenty Three

They rose and joined Zach and Jessica outside in the corridor leading to the lobby. At the far end, a slow mob of groaning, ragged figures were shambling together.

"They're coming this way," Zach said with glee. "They look great."

"Zombies," said Detective Martin flatly. "I'm pretty sure that's my cue to actually go off duty, like I was supposed to six hours ago. See you guys tomorrow."

"Freaking zombies," muttered Daniel. "Cluttering up survival horror. Nobody does *Silent Hill* anymore, it's all *Walking Dead*. Goodnight, Anne."

"Are the zombies coming?" Rita came toward them, munching from a bag of M&Ms. "Oh, there they are! I was afraid I'd miss it."

"Not likely," Zach assured her. "There's too many to miss. It'll be a full-scale apocalypse in here."

"As exciting as that sounds," Daniel said, "I'm exhausted, too. I'll see you guys in the morning." He gave them a tired wave and headed to the escalators.

Dozens of zombies, from *The Walking Dead* and *28 Days Later* and *The Last of Us* and *World War Z* and more, Jacob supposed, and even some Reavers from *Firefly* had sneaked in. All were staggering down the hall, moaning and reaching out at the other attendees who leapt back, laughing. Most were moving slowly, but a few quick zombies zigged among them, making poorly-aimed grabs.

"It's an impressive bunch of zombies," Sam said. She frowned. "What do we call a group of zombies? You know, like a herd of deer, a murder of crows, a crash of rhinos — is it a shuffle of zombies? What are they?"

"A horde," said Zach.

"I kind of like 'shuffle,'" said Jessica.

"Shouldn't it be a plague of zombies?" suggested Jacob.

"I saw 'a thriller of zombies' once online," said Rita.

Several of the zombies showed off stunning special effects makeup. One appeared to be leaking intestines as she moved, while another's face seemed to peel back at the mouth, revealing teeth and a bit of bloody skull. "Ew," said Rita. "I hope nobody leaves anything messy that the hotel can fine us for."

Jacob cupped his hands about his mouth. "Take only victims, leave only terror! No body parts or blood left behind!"

A handful of zombies bobbed agreement or snarled, and the spectators laughed. Cameras and cell phones were flashing all along the hall.

A group shuffled together as a variety pack from *Plants vs Zombies*, wearing traffic cones and snorkeling gear. One even straddled an inflatable dolphin pool toy, bobbing along the hallway in little porpoising leaps.

"Look! Look at that!" Jessica bounced and pointed.

Two zombies lurched down the hallway, placards on their chests reading *Enormous hair* and *Nice kilt you're wearing*. Beside them crept a man in a grey suit, wearing an old game console as a backpack and a QWERTY keyboard slung from his shoulders, ready for action.

"It's *Typing of the Dead!*" Jessica laughed. "That's brilliant. Really brilliant."

A zombie pushed through the line and grabbed at a *Left 4 Dead* Boomer, who snarled and shoved him away with a flap of meaty arms. The zombie clutched at its artfully-torn throat and reached for the Witch beside the Boomer, leaving a streak of faux blood on her arm. The Witch recoiled and then slashed with her claws, and the Boomer shoved him again.

"I guess there's still tribalism even after death," Jessica observed. "Zombies of a feather shuffle together."

"Technically, the *Left 4 Dead* infected aren't really dead," Zach said.

The zombie with the cut throat reeled to the side of the hall, making several onlookers scatter with little laughing shrieks. A photographer crouched and snapped several quick shots of its outstretched arm. It turned with a little gurgling moan.

"Ooh, that's kind of gruesome," Jessica said approvingly. "Well done."

The zombie turned and lunged at them, moaning and bubbling, and they jumped away, laughing. It snatched at Sam but she pulled free. Its groan rose in pitch.

"Seriously?" Rita was annoyed. "Fake blood all down her arm. He's just lucky he missed her costume. What's wrong with people?"

The zombie flailed and looked around and upward, wailing wordlessly.

"Jacob." Sam's voice was cold and taut. He turned to her, seeing her roll the syrup blood on her fingers. "Jacob, this blood's warm."

Jacob stared at her a second, and then he turned back to the stumbling zombie. "Hey!" He started forward, reaching for its arm. "Are you okay?"

For the first time he looked at the zombie's eyes, and they were wide, the pupils dilated. Beneath the special effects makeup, he was terrified. He held one hand to his throat, and now Jacob could see the thick red blood was seeping from the wound, which was deeper than a special effects prosthetic could manage.

Jacob called over his shoulder, "Call 911! We need an ambulance!" and drew the zombie to the side of the hall. Beside them, the rest of the zombies shuffled onward, moaning and snarling.

"I need a bandage." Jacob glanced around and then pulled his Con Aid shirt over his head, pressing it into the zombie's neck. It stuck immediately. He pressed the zombie gently to the floor, so that he sat against the wall. "Who's on the phone? Do we have someone?"

Sam crouched beside him. "Severe throat wound, bleeding pretty hard," she reported into her phone. "Also bleeding from the mouth, maybe the nose. Hard to see through the special effects makeup."

The zombie gestured to his neck, and Jacob caught his hand. "You sit still. You've been moving too much for that kind of injury. Stay still."

The zombie's wide eyes met his, and Jacob's stomach twisted.

"Eight minutes," he said, picking a number he hoped wasn't too far from the truth. "That's all we need. You just sit here, very still, and we'll take care of you until they get here." He half-turned his head, speaking to the others but keeping his eyes on the frightened zombie. "We need some blankets."

Rita was gone, probably to the front desk. Jessica drew off her heavy cloak and laid it over the zombie. "Here."

The zombie's mouth worked, but the slipping facial prostheses confused the movement of his lips. "Shh," Jacob said. "Be still. Try to relax." It was a silly thing to say, but he could feel the zombie's racing pulse through the saturated t-shirt as the heart tried to compensate for the lost blood.

Rita came back, accompanied by two hotel security guards. One knelt with a first aid kit as the other spread blankets across the zombie's lap and torso.

"Don't remove the shirt," cautioned Jacob as the first drew bandages from the kit.

"I know." She tore open sterile packaging and began to press gauze over the dark shirt.

The zombie's breath was slowing now, too, and his head leaned heavily against the wall. Jacob looked at him. Would the ambulance be in time?

This hadn't been an accident. Jacob leaned to face the zombie directly. "Who did this?" he asked. "Do you know who did this to you?"

The zombie's eyes fluttered, and his mouth worked. Jacob could make out nothing. If he didn't make it…. Getting a dying statement was unpleasant for all involved, but this might be their only chance to interview the victim.

He concentrated on choosing his words. "Do you understand that this is a very serious injury? That you're dying?"

The wide, frightened eyes stared at him and the torn face bobbed slightly.

"Can you tell us who it was?"

The mouth moved again, but with his severed throat, he could not speak, and his bloodied lips and slipping prosthetics blurred his weak whisper.

"Shove over," Zach said, appearing and kneeling on the other side.

The zombie spoke again, his stiff multi-layered lips and extra teeth slick with blood, and then he blinked at Zach.

"I got part of that," Zach said, more gently than Jacob

had ever heard him speak. "Can you say it again?"

The zombie's eyes closed, but his mouth repeated the movements, and a little gurgle came from beneath the bloody shirt.

Zach glanced at Jacob, worried, and then the wail of sirens broke over the sounds of the zombie gathering. "There, you hear that?" Jacob said to the zombie. "They're here. Now just hold on."

The zombie's eyes closed and his fingers tightened on Jacob's wrist.

Chapter Twenty Four

The wounded zombie, despite the EMTs' epinephrine and blood, did not survive the ambulance ride to the hospital.

The police were frustrated and their tempers were short. "How can no one have seen where he came from?" a uniformed man asked. He'd arrived shortly after the EMTs. "Nobody just appears in the middle of a hotel convention center with his throat cut. Where did it happen, and how did he get here?"

"The whole place was full of zombies," Jacob said. "It was a big event. I'll bet there were hundreds of zombies in the halls."

"And lots of them were bloody and disfigured, and one more just blended right in," Daniel said grimly. His escape to his room hadn't lasted long. Now he wore jeans and a Darth Vader t-shirt. Jacob's shirt had gone in the ambulance with the zombie, and he had gotten another Con Aid shirt from the Con Ops office, which hung too loose and too long on him.

"It was freaking ingenious," Lydia put in, "if the killer wanted to cut the guy and buy himself time to get away. Everyone just thought he was part of the show until it was too late. Really sick, but ingenious."

She'd come to join them as word spread through the con. This wasn't like a rumor of a death by poisoning; this had been public and bloody, and hundreds of people had seen the gory zombie rushed through the lobby and into the ambulance. People were afraid, she'd reported.

"He lasted a long time, they said," Detective Martin offered, coming into the staff suite. "He'd been bleeding for a while, and he stayed up longer than most would with that kind of wound. It might be that the killer didn't think he'd even make it that far, and maybe he was supposed to be found hours later in some other place. No wallet or ID on him, so either it was robbery or it was supposed to look like it."

"What do we think happened?"

"Too early to say for sure, but preliminary is that he was hit in the face at least once, with an object or fist or something blunt, and then his throat was cut. Could have been from front or behind, we won't know until the ME has a chance to get a better look."

"And that blow or blows loosened or moved the facial prosthetics, which is what made it so hard to understand him whispering." Daniel nodded. "That makes sense. That, and that his larynx was cut." He turned to Zach. "But you say you got something."

Zach nodded. "Jacob asked him who'd done it, and I went over to help."

"Hold on," said Detective Martin. "Sorry, I just got here, and I'm already exhausted. Who are you, and why did you think you could help?"

"I'm Zach Hu, and I do speech therapy," Zach said. "I've put a lot of hours into studying visemes."

"And what's a viseme?"

"The position of your mouth and face when you make a sound. Like this is *oooooooh*." He pointed to his rounded lips.

"And so you were able to understand the dying man?"

Zach shook his head. "They tell us that less than half of English phonetics are distinguishable by viseme alone, and a lot of sounds look alike. I can narrow it down, but that's it."

"Well, give us what it's narrowed down to."

"He had an R sound, and then either a F or a V — they look identical. And there was another syllable, with what I think was a T or a D."

"That's it?"

"What with the weird makeup and the reduced lip movement as he was slowing down, that's pretty good," Zach answered. "Sorry, but that's the best I can do."

"You told him you got most of it!" Jacob protested.

"And asked him to repeat it, yes," Zach said. "I didn't want him frustrated, because when people try to exaggerate they usually make it harder to read, not easier."

"Still, that gives us something to work with," Detective Martin said. "Now, who did he know with the initials RFT or RVD?"

Daniel shook his head. "Might not have been a person. We're at a con, and we call things by what they look like. Those could be a reference to something in a game or movie, just like an AT-ST or R2-D2. Or it might not be initials, if Zach missed the bits in between."

"There was definitely stuff in between," Zach confirmed.

"So they might be part of a name. Like R-something Aff Taksaorn, or Prince Vandersnooten."

"Who?"

"Doesn't matter, the point is we aren't necessarily looking for initials. And if he didn't know his attacker's name, he might have tried to describe him, and we could be looking for a character, or a creature type, or even some mundane in a Red Formal Tux."

"'Prince Vandersnooten' doesn't start with an R," said Jessica.

"But it's got an R sound. Could it work that way?"

Daniel looked at Zach.

"Given that he wasn't speaking normally, yeah, there could have been an initial phoneme or two that I couldn't catch. I'm sorry. I really did try."

"We know you did, Zach," Jessica said. "Nobody thinks anything else."

Detective Martin put her hands to her temples. "I hate this thing," she said. "More specifically, I hate this guy. If it's the same guy, I hate him, and I'm going to take off work to sit through every day of his trial and eat popcorn as he gets sentenced." She exhaled forcefully. "Okay, what do we do?"

"First off, we keep people safe," Vince said. "Even if that means taking steps none of us want to take. But people's lives are more important. Detective Martin, do you think it would be better if we shut the convention down?"

Detective Martin pressed her fingers against the inside corners of her eyebrows. "No," she said after a long moment. "I don't think so. I agree with you about people's lives, absolutely, but I don't feel like these are random acts. There should be a pattern or process, if we can just get to it."

"And sending everyone home would scatter our witnesses as well as the suspect," Daniel added. "It's one thing to let people go home from a party or theater, and another to let them spread over five or eight states."

Vince nodded, more than a little relieved. "Good. I mean, I don't want anyone else to get hurt, obviously, but to be honest I didn't want to shut down the con either. It would be tough, after that."

Detective Martin sighed again. "Okay, people, this is your turf. What do you suggest? What's the best way to get people to talk?"

There was a moment of quiet, and then Jacob said, "Just

ask. They've already seen the ambulances and heard about the deaths; they're not going to panic any more than they already are. Telling them the investigation is underway and being taken seriously is the best way to get help out of them."

"They're likely to be friendly?" she asked, glancing at Daniel.

"These are geeks," he answered. "There are exceptions, anyone can be a fan, but for the most part you're looking at white collar, middle-class, clean records. Definitely some drinking going on in the hotel rooms, probably some other stuff in the dance crowd, but for the most part your more serious offenders have a longer string of speeding tickets. You're not going to get as much kick against the man here."

"So we can put out an official request and let uniforms take statements?"

"Should work fine."

"Okay, then. Let's get this on the news — or better, on whatever internal messaging you have for the con, the app or Twitter or whatever."

"Both of those," Vince confirmed. "And we've been seeing a lot of photos tweeted in, so I'm sure you're getting a lot of photos uploaded to the police account. So people are willing to help, if they think they have anything that could be helpful."

"Don't get lost," Daniel said to Zach. "You took a dying statement."

"What's that mean?"

"It's the only time hearsay evidence is ever admissible in court. That is, if it's taken right." He looked at Jacob.

Jacob straightened. "I asked if he knew he was dying and if he could tell us who had done it."

"And?"

"He nodded."

"Once or twice?"

Jacob thought. "It was fast, but I think he nodded to each. Little nods, he was pretty weak."

"That should hold up, then. Good thinking. Now we just have to work out this RFD thing." He frowned. "Could that be it? A radio frequency device?"

"Killed by a glorified pager?" Detective Martin sighed. "I'm keeping my mind open on this one. First time I've seen a zombie murdered, and the first time I've been interviewing fictional characters." She stood. "Oh, how I'll be glad to get out of these shoes. Long, long day. Vince, how do we get the word out?"

"You give us the wording, we'll upload it."

"Good. I'll be back shortly."

People scattered, going for coffee or just to move around and release some tension. Jacob rotated his phone in his hands.

"You can help with this, Jacob," came Lydia's voice behind him. "This is your territory. You've got Knowledge Local."

He gave her a weak smile. "It's not exactly a role-playing game, Aunt Lydia."

"Most of life is, actually," she said. "Don't try to reinvent the wheel in thinking about the investigation they're doing. They're good at that, and you're not going to be able to contribute much when they don't have to share their info with you. But they aren't geeks, and this is a geek murder. That's your ground. Don't be afraid to follow, you know, hunches."

"Use the Force?"

"That too."

He sighed. "I'll try. But man, this is hard. I mean, that guy practically died in my arms."

Lydia leaned over to hug him. "You okay? I mean, not that you can be, but are you managing?"

"I'll be okay. I just want to end this. No more deaths."

She squeezed him again. "No more deaths. End this."

"Hey, Jacob?" Sam called over the pass-through. "Can I borrow a few bucks? It sounds wrong to say I want to eat after that, but… I need food. Blood sugar's wonky."

"Sure." Jacob pulled his wallet from his pocket and tossed it to her. "I think Vince was trying to get some pizzas ordered, but I don't know how successful he was. There's probably some mac and cheese or something left at one of the upper tables. I don't think they were getting as much traffic."

"Thanks."

"I'll come with you," Lydia said. "Chocolate isn't a panacea, but it fakes one pretty well." She headed out the door.

"Vince?" Daniel came in, accompanied by Detective Martin. "Can we speak with you a moment?"

The con chair looked up, his expression worried and then resigned. "Yeah, sure. Rita, don't go — if this is going where I think it is, I want you to hear it."

Chapter Twenty Five

"So, Vince." Detective Martin's expression was gentle but firm. "Tell us about the financial state of the con."

Vince interlaced his fingers and set his elbows on the table. "It wasn't supposed to work out like this."

"It rarely is. Tell us what went wrong."

Jacob sat very still. No one had asked him to leave, and Vince seemed resigned to openness, but there was no point to taking chances.

"Con Job has been running for eight years. It's done pretty well for itself; the con has been self-sufficient for five years. It's been making enough money to even pay a little bit to the key staffers, the department heads."

"Is that unusual?"

"Depends on the con. Some of your biggest cons or industry cons have paid staff, but a lot of the smaller and middling cons are all volunteer-run. That is, they have staff, and they have volunteers, but the staff don't get paid, either."

"What makes someone staff, then?"

"Higher position, more authority, and some perks — staff get comped rooms at the hotel, shared, and meals in the staff suite. When we have one." He gestured to encompass the stripped room around them.

"So Con Job was in the black. What happened?"

Vince sighed. "I sort of borrowed some money. But it would have been fine if we hadn't been robbed."

"If you use words like 'sort of borrowed' and 'robbed,'

I'm going to have to ask you to explain further."

"Yes, I took some money out of Con Job's accounts for my personal use. It was kind of owed to me, you know? I've been chairing this con for six years, I basically got it to this level, and I hadn't ever been paid, not really. Last year I got a check for seventy-eight dollars. That's not a lot for thousands of man-hours."

"Couldn't you have asked for more payment?"

"Yeah, but…. No one chairs a con to make money. We do it for the fans. It would have looked bad."

"It looks a lot worse when you just embezzle it."

"Embezzling is stealing," Vince said quickly. "I wasn't stealing. I was borrowing. It was going to go back in the con's account before anyone realized it was missing."

Rita shook her head. "Vince, when you borrow something without asking permission, especially money, that's called stealing."

Jacob glanced at Daniel, who looked strained and sad.

"I needed liquid funds. I was going to put it back. We would have been fine if not for Ted."

"Who's Ted?"

"He's the vice-chair," Rita said, looking perplexed, "or was. He quit, which was kind of a nightmare right before the con. We were all upset with him, but Vince said to just let him go."

Vince rubbed at his forehead. "Ted had made withdrawals, too. And he'd done a lot of other things for a while, charging in expenses to the con for his own services and products. Some of it wasn't anything we could really prosecute for, like he rewrote a single line in our guest contract and charged Con Job almost a thousand dollars in consulting fees. That's not actually illegal, just really slimy.

We were just as well off without him."

"And was it all legal but underhanded stuff?"

"No." Vince sighed. "He also made withdrawals on the con account. And he wasn't intending to pay them back."

"But you couldn't press charges against him without bringing your own withdrawals to light."

"Right. And I didn't have the money paid back yet. And he knew I couldn't do anything about him, and he said he'd counter-accuse me if anyone from the con tried to go after him legally. So I thought we could hold the con as usual, I could pay back the money, and then I'd look at the accounts and see if we could press charges."

"So," said Detective Martin, "you and this Ted both took money from the con funds, so neither of you could accuse the other without risking exposure of your own embezzlement."

This time Vince didn't protest the word. "Basically, yeah. Only I was really going to pay the con back. Ted took thousands. Tens of thousands. It was after the con last year, when I took out the money. We had time before we would need to make any new payments, it seemed like the best time to do it. But Ted noticed, and when I said I was going to pay everything back before it was missed, he said I couldn't prove that and he could report me to the rest of the staff and press charges. But he wasn't going to, he said, because he was just going to do it too, and I couldn't do anything about it."

"So he did."

"It was a nightmare. He took so much more, and it was never coming back. So I had to cut costs in any way I could, and I made a big deal about getting corporate sponsorship this year."

"That's why you made us go back to the dark ages with our registration system," Rita said.

"And a lot of other things, like less food in the green room and a lighter staff suite and a whole host of other things. Oh, man, it was killer, trying to keep it hidden from everyone."

"I hope not," said Detective Martin pointedly.

Vince looked at her. "Oh, no. No, I didn't kill anyone. I wouldn't. I couldn't."

"Really? Because it sounds like Valerie Kimberton's sponsorship with MEGAN!ME was your ticket off the nightmare coaster, and then she threatened to pull her sponsorship, and then she ended up dead."

"I didn't kill her," Vince said firmly. "I'm not sorry she's dead, and maybe it's wrong of me to say that, and maybe stupid of me to say it, but I didn't kill her."

"Tell me how Valerie Kimberton fit in."

"You're right, she and MEGAN!ME were a big part of getting Con Job afloat. It seemed like a reasonable deal: MEGAN!ME got the back cover, the inside front cover, three interior ad spaces, a lot of mentions in the copy and programming, and special vendor space. We even have a MEGAN!ME video track showing their featured titles running nonstop in one video room all weekend. She got plenty of exposure for her money."

"People say she was hard to work with."

Vince snorted. "That's a pretty minimalist way to say it."

"Why did she threaten to pull her sponsorship?"

"Which time?"

Detective Martin's pen hesitated. "She did it more than once?"

"Oh, yeah. On Friday she was mad about a typo in the programs — the exclamation mark was left out of the

MEGAN!ME name, in an article. Not even in an ad or a headline, but in a write-up. It shouldn't have been anything but a mistake, but she wanted all-new programs printed." He shrugged. "By then I wasn't taking her quite so seriously. She'd scared me a lot worse before, when she threatened to pull out a month ago and then again last week. That was over an article, which we dropped from the program book to make her happy, and then because we were giving *The Last Days of Manhattan* a featured viewing, and it's not a MEGAN!ME title. Like it was suddenly a MEGAN!ME con, all MEGAN!ME all the time, which wasn't ever the deal."

"So you weren't really afraid she was going to pull the money and walk?"

"Well, yeah, at first I was. And then still a little bit on Friday, because I figured she had dirty lawyers who could argue that the MEGAN!ME brand had been misrepresented or something, and Con Job sure didn't have money to fight. Our only lawyer-type was the paralegal who had taken our money and run." Vince seemed a little more sure of himself now that they were speaking of Valerie and not his own crimes. "But I didn't kill her."

"Did you want to?"

"And give her dirty lawyers something else to hold over us? She's the kind of person who'd be thrilled from beyond the grave to nail us with a wrongful death suit or something. No way."

Daniel cleared his throat and spoke for the first time. "Why'd you take the money, Vince?"

Vince's expression seemed to melt into sadness and regret. "I needed it. For Charlie. And I was going to pay it back."

"Who's Charlie?" asked Detective Martin, but Daniel and Rita had already subtly changed their postures.

Rita's eyebrows drew in and upward. "Charlie?"

Vince nodded once, and then he answered Detective Martin. "My son. My ex-wife has him. He's got — he's got some problems. Insurance wouldn't cover it, said his autism is medical but behavior problems aren't covered. And he needed some specialized help."

"What'd you do?"

"I took enough to pay for a few sessions with a therapist. She sent Charlie to work with a specialist, someone who could work with him and — it's going good. They think he can get into a special program at school, which is amazing progress, and last time I visited him he even wanted to click me with his little clicker." He swallowed. "It was worth it. Totally worth it. And I'm paying it back, about seventy-five percent now. I only took a few thousand, to pay for the sessions and Terri's gas and hotel — that's my ex-wife — and money so she could take off work to go with him. It's mostly back already."

Daniel swore. "Why didn't you just ask for help, man?"

Vince's head drooped. "Who's got six thousand dollars sitting around? Who would just lend it to someone, if they did?"

"You might be surprised," Daniel said sadly.

Rita ran a finger beneath one eye. "You were talking about you and Terri the other day," she said. "How things were better."

"Yeah." Vince swallowed. "We — that is — we'd never tell him, of course, but Charlie was.... It was really hard, living with a special needs kid, and we didn't know how to do it. Not at first. And we split. But after Charlie got help, and Terri says she's been learning a lot about how to teach him, and we... it's been better. A lot better. And Terri said she'd like to see us maybe try things out again."

"That's going to be hard if you're in prison," Daniel said heavily. "Man, Vince...."

"I know. I know. You don't even have to tell me. I'm sorry." He rubbed at his forehead again. "But for Charlie. I had to."

"That's all we'll need from you at the moment," Detective Martin said, a little sharply. "Thank you. Rita, you can go, too."

Vince rose and walked from the room, not looking back, and Rita followed.

Detective Martin swore and threw her pen at the ground. "Am I supposed to be the cop who built her career on the guy who stole to get his autistic kid an education and then was even paying it back? Oh, there's no good way out of this one."

Daniel sighed. "Nope."

Detective Martin glanced at Jacob. "And I don't think he's our murderer, anyway. He only had to ride out Kimberton a little bit longer, so if he snapped and killed her, it would have been an act of impulse violence, not something premeditated like poison. And it doesn't do a thing to explain Kurlansky and our latest victim, the dead zombie."

"The guy's a friend of mine, so I might be biased," said Daniel, "but I think you're right." He looked at Jacob. "Got any ideas?"

Jacob blew out his breath. "Everybody's got something here," he said. "But most of them aren't killing for it, I don't think."

"All it takes is one," sighed Detective Martin. "Man, I hope he can get that money back in the bank before this settles. It'd be great to have nothing missing when it comes up."

"But he—" Jacob stopped himself. "He didn't confess anything. He just talked with us."

"And anything we repeat would be hearsay," she agreed, "not admissible as evidence. If the money's all back, the case would be dropped, and I wouldn't be the baddest bad cop of all time." She rolled her eyes. "Like not having kids yet isn't enough — if my mom and aunts found out I'd booked a guy for taking care of his autistic kid, I'd have to change my name."

"Yeah."

Jacob's stomach rumbled, and he wondered how long it had been since dinner. Had he had dinner? He couldn't remember. There had been the Expecto Pastrami from the food truck, but had he eaten since then?

"I think I'll get something from the snack table, too," he said. He stood and stopped. "Oh, Sam's got my wallet."

"You can catch her," said Detective Martin. "Unless things have significantly changed, she'll still be in line."

"You guys want anything?"

"A perp in cuffs," said Detective Martin.

Chapter Twenty Six

Jacob saw Sam and Lydia from the escalator. They waved to him, holding bags of M&Ms, and he waved back and jogged to meet them. "You're through! Detective Martin thought you'd still be in line."

"Yeah, they're being pretty efficient. Necessity, I guess. But it sounds like they'll be out of stuff soon."

"Vince was trying to order pizzas, so maybe they'll come soon. Can I have my wallet? I want to grab something, too."

Sam looked at him. "I don't have it."

"I gave it to you downstairs, remember?"

"And I took five bucks out and left it on the counter, where you put it." Her eyes widened. "I'm sorry, I thought you saw me."

"Better hurry," Lydia said.

Jacob turned and ran down the opposite escalator — though that was silly, and if the wallet were gone then hurrying wouldn't change that. He sprinted across the lobby and reached the Con Ops room, and there was the wallet, brown and rubbed and creased, lying on the pass-through.

Daniel looked up at him, and Jacob held it up. "Kind of needed this."

He held up the wallet to Sam and Lydia, riding the escalator down, and they cheered. He had just made it to the mezzanine again when his phone buzzed. He glanced down to find a text from Jessica. *OMG, is it true?*

*That depends on what *it* is,* he wrote back. *Pluto is no longer a planet. There is no Santa Claus.*

A moment later his phone rang. "Oh, you're hilarious," Jessica laughed, "but you're not getting out of it that easily. I mean the picture."

"What picture?"

"Have you seriously not seen it yet?"

"I've been a little busy here, Jessica, what with the con and the murders and the creepers and the zombies and all."

"Fine, I get it. I'm talking about — oh, hang on, I'm coming down."

She hung up, and Jacob mentally shrugged. If Jessica couldn't find a legitimate cause, she'd invent one. She was always getting excited about something.

"Jacob, can you go out and meet the pizza guy?" Vince called. "He's going to need help."

"We got pizza?"

"I found a place that would deliver. I paid online, delivery and tip too, so you just have to get them to all the food stations."

"Right."

There wasn't one pizza guy at the hotel entrance, but two, with pizza boxes stacked high on hotel luggage carts. "You must be having one helluva party," one said.

"We're trying," Jacob answered. "If you'll push those after me, we can drop them off where they belong."

The hotel had provided paper plates, stacked on each table. Waiting attendees cheered from their line as Jacob led the pizzas to the first table. The delivery guys looked startled, and then they strutted and raised their arms for the applause.

They left a dozen each of cheese and pepperoni pizzas at the first station, and another set at the second. By the time they had delivered the last, the first station's line was halfway gone but the remaining attendees looked worried. "Is there gonna be enough?" they could hear someone call. "Should we go to another table?"

"You're gonna need more pizzas," said one of the delivery drivers.

"It was hard enough getting you guys," Jacob said. "I get the feeling we're kind of the only all-night convention that comes to this town. There's just nothing around here open at night."

"Yeah," agreed the pizza guys. "Maybe we could ask the manager to call out. There's got to be some locations further out that would be willing to drive in. I mean how often do you get to move eight dozen pizzas at a single sale?"

"Or maybe they'd just spot us the supplies. We were pretty tapped out after this; we were supposed to get restocked on Monday."

"If you talk to him and if he can swing anything, let us know," Jacob said. "I'm sure we'd be happy to get more if we can."

"You got it," the delivery guys said. "Tip on eight dozen pizzas isn't too shabby, either."

They waved and headed out the door. Jacob turned back into the lobby and nearly stumbled into Ryan Brazil. "Oh, sorry."

"Me, too, Jacob." Ryan smiled a tight little smile.

"What?"

"About what goes around coming around."

Jacob tipped his head. "I'm not following."

"You seemed to think it was fine to look over my shoulder and peek at my stuff. So I thought I'd take a peek at yours. Only fair, right?"

"I didn't...."

"So I took a glance at your wallet, when you left it so conveniently available, and I was hoping I'd find something really juicy. But it was just your driver's license and credit card. Pretty boring, you'd think — except yours wasn't."

Jacob's stomach tightened. "What are you talking about?"

"It's a different name than the one on your badge. Why is that, I wondered. And why was the name Jacob Tarston so familiar? And it was right on the edge of my brain, I just couldn't remember."

Jacob's stomach finished tightening and started twisting. "Leave it alone, Ryan."

"Oh, it's too late for that. You should have left it alone before you started talking to the police about my perfectly legal friendship with an adult woman." He pointed a finger at Jacob's face. "It would have saved you a lot of trouble."

The words were hard to form. "What did you do?"

"I remembered. I remembered spending a lot of days watching bad TV, eating cup ramen and hoping for a job. I remembered a dreadful little show about fat slutty women and their bratty, dysfunctional men — and a bratty, dysfunctional kid."

Jacob stopped breathing.

"Have you really not noticed yet? I went to the front desk, asked them to put up a birthday message. They're so upset by all the weird stuff about the kitchens and the food, they were more than happy to help do something nice for one of the con personnel. Your happy birthday is running on every agenda screen, every map, every in-room closed-circuit TV, pretty much every public screen on this hotel."

Jacob tore his eyes from the grinning face and turned to scan the lobby. There, over the green couch, a large screen.

Welcome, Con Job! it read. And as he watched, the screen split into vertical panels which rotated to the next message. *We deeply regret the inconvenience of our closed kitchens. Packaged foods are available at tables in the lobby, the convention center main hall, and on the mezzanine.*

And then the screen split and rotated again, and Jacob's face appeared, happy and smiling, his profile picture online. *Happy Birthday to Jacob Foster, once Little Jakey Tarston!* And beside that, an impossibly real photo from the past, a light-haired little boy with a twisted expression and one hand raised to the camera, the offending digit pixelated out but plainly inferable.

"Oh, there you are!" Jessica's voice rang down to him, and he looked up. She was leaning over the railing on the mezzanine. "I've been looking for you. Have you seen it yet? Is it true? Everybody's talking about it!" She laughed.

So did Ryan. "The only articles I could find said you'd left the family, tried to leave all that behind," he said. "Nothing's ever left behind, Jakey. Nothing."

Jacob wanted to hit him, wanted to shove that smug evil grin up behind his nose and knock him to the floor, but his arms wouldn't move. Ryan turned and strutted away, still chuckling, and Jessica's phone flashed from the mezzanine. "Say cheese! Everyone online wants a pic. They're all so surprised!"

Chapter Twenty Seven

Jacob pushed back the Con Ops door and dropped into a chair, but not because he wanted to. His body seemed to acting on auto-pilot and without his consent. He didn't want to be in Con Ops. He didn't want to be near anyone he was working with, people who liked him and maybe respected him and maybe, maybe would have given him good references when he was up for Academy admission.

But his body wasn't listening to him, and it sat in Con Ops and stared at the photoshoot schedule as if it mattered.

"You okay, Jacob?" someone called, but he barely registered the words, much less who had said them. His phone buzzed — had been buzzing at irregular intervals — but he ignored it.

And then the door burst open. "Jake!" Sam stepped inside, scanned for him, started toward him. "Jacob, I just saw — I can't — I can't even...."

"Hey, is this for real?" Paul asked, staring at his tablet. "Our feed is going crazy with tweets about you being Little Jakey Tarston. Is that true?"

Jacob whirled, jolting the chair from beneath him. He started toward Paul, ready to tear the tablet from him and smash it to the floor, grinding the pieces into the industrial carpet.

Sam flung her messenger bag to the floor and took a step to reach the folding table of snacks for the Ops team. She swept the table surface, scattering pizza boxes and energy bars across the room. "What is wrong with all of you? Why are you in here talking about Twitter when there's a creeper out there creeping on innocent kids?"

The room went quiet, and Jacob froze with the rest. Then Paul said, "Now just calm down a second. What are you talking about?"

"The same guy who was getting pictures of me is also getting pictures of minors. I think the con's in enough trouble already, right? And that's not going to sit well with anyone."

"No, it's not," Paul said. He turned his head to Daniel. "Does Con Aid know about this?"

"We do," answered Daniel, "although we'd be very interested to know what new information Sam has for us. Sam, Jacob, will you take a walk with me to the staff suite?"

They followed him to the other room. Jacob glanced at Sam and then looked away before their eyes could meet. She reached out and tightened her fingers briefly about his wrist.

Daniel held the door as they entered the staff suite and then shut it behind them. He turned to face them. "Okay, get it out, whatever it really is."

Sam turned and pulled Jacob close, her arms squeezing about his shoulders. "I am so sorry. I am so, so sorry. I just saw."

His arms rose mechanically to embrace her in return.

She held him a moment and then let him go. "You okay?"

"In there…."

"Yeah, you had a bad look on your face. I figured it would be better for everyone if we didn't find out where it was going."

"Yeah. Probably. So, thank you."

She shrugged. "Meh. What's the point of being a

hysterical female if I can't use it to somebody's advantage once in a while?"

"While I appreciate what you did," Daniel interjected gently, "you might want to go back and help with the cleanup. Also, is what you said about the minor true?"

"Yep. I just talked to another girl from the voice contest, who was all excited that he'd approached her with the same skeevy line about keeping in touch and he could drop her name to the right people." Her jaw muscles tightened. "I hope his pants get dry-cleaned and shrink while he's still in them."

"Detective Martin will be glad to know about the minor — not glad, per se, or not glad about the creeping, but glad that it's a lot easier to do something about that." Daniel nodded. "I foresee an unpleasant few days in Brazil's future. In the meantime, do you mind if I have a word with Jacob?"

Jacob's stomach sank. The numbness was fading from him, and it was a horrid first sensation.

"Sure," Sam said with only a hint of reluctance. She looked at Jacob, and he gave her a weak smile. She deserved one.

And then she left, and he was alone with Daniel, the weight of unspoken questions hanging heavy over them.

Daniel took a few steps away to straddle a chair. "So, what about this?"

"I'm... not Jacob Foster." He sat down and looked at the floor. "I started using my aunt's name when I went to live with her. She and my mom were half-sisters." He was just delaying, he knew it. He glanced at Daniel and then looked away. "My real name is Jacob Tarston. And yes, I really was Little Jakey on *Cougars and Cold Ones*."

There was a silence, and at last he looked again at Daniel. The big policeman was still, just looking at him.

"Wow," he said finally. "You just kind of forget those might be real people, I guess."

"They're not," Jacob said, "not by the time the reality TV machine is done with them. My family was paid to be even crazier than they started, which was plenty. Mom wasn't allowed to see her therapist while we were shooting, they used to tell different people different script scenarios to confuse us, they used to leave cases of beer outside the door just to make sure.... So much of that stuff was staged, but not in any way that felt like — we weren't actors, you know? We were set up. We were one long prank being played on ourselves, only Mom signed us up for it and rolled right along with all of it." He shook his head. "That was all fine for her, I guess, but I was a kid. I had no say in it, and she sold off my identity and any future I had."

Daniel nodded once. "But you got out."

"Aunt Lydia did all that. She knew I was going to be stuck under that forever — Little Jakey Tarston, the Beer Boy whose butt got pixelated out on daytime television. How would I ever get a decent job with that on my resume? What about college? And...."

"And the Academy."

"The psychological exam. Now you know why I was worried." Jacob swallowed. "A stable background, they want. No history of mental illness or irrational behavior." He threw up his hands helplessly. "And I mooned old women in syndication while my mother threw beer cans at her boyfriend-of-the-week's car. It's a career-killer before I even start."

Daniel drew a slow, audible breath. "Yep, that one would require some discussion with the shrinks."

Jacob rested his head in his hands. "Aunt Lydia's the

only reason I'm out of all that. As soon as the show got canceled and the family wasn't backed by the network lawyers, she tore into them with tooth and nail. She hit them with neglect, endangerment, something about lack of education, I don't even know, she was a lawyer on fire. The rest of the family was hating all over her — I think now they were hoping to get picked up by the network again — and she pretty much didn't care.

"Mom caved, finally. I think she saw that the court was probably going to grant custody to Aunt Lydia if it came to their decision, and if that happened, Mom would have no say over me and she couldn't drag me back if the show ever got picked up again. So she stopped fighting and I went to live with Aunt Lydia. We're still working on changing my name legally, because of the way the trust was set up, but I can use another name for everything that isn't legal stuff. So I call myself Jacob Foster most of the time. My driver's license still reads Jacob Tarston, but it's not like I have to show that to everyone."

"So your aunt got you out."

"She got me away from them, and she got a share of what we were paid put in trust for me. Which was really smart, because Mom and them of course blew through it all in a couple of years, and every once in a while I get a phone call or an email about how they need money and it's not fair that I have an account full of cash I'm not even using. Like it doesn't matter that it's paying for my education, so I don't have to live like that." He shrugged. "I'm just telling you this now because I know I'm lucky that I got out. I am. But… I wanted to make it a little further. To take my fresh name out and make it my own, prove that I can be what I want to be without that following me."

"And you're worried that it won't happen."

"Now that everyone knows who I am? Who I was?"

"Not everyone," Daniel corrected gently. "Some people, at one event."

Jacob tried to smile and couldn't manage it. "You say that like Twitter and Facebook and Tumblr don't exist. Little Jakey Tarston appears at a geek convention with multiple murders? You think no one's going to grab on to that detail in a news story? I guess I can hope for a nuclear strike or something to draw off attention, but I don't think it's going to happen."

Daniel sighed. "Unfortunately, I think you're right. It's not news unless it has a celebrity name in it." He folded his hands. "But — I know my perspective on this is different than yours, but that's an advantage right now. I know this seems like the biggest thing in the world, like it's your whole life. Because it *is* your whole life, so that only makes sense. But it's not everyone else's life, and I don't think they're going to look at it the same way."

Jacob eyed him warily. "What do you mean?"

"I mean people are selfish, egotistical little entertainment-seeking missiles, and if it's not about them or amusing them, they forget about it like absent-minded goldfish on meth." He shrugged. "So even if the story breaks, you sit tight and keep your head down, and don't give them any drama. Don't fight, don't argue about what they've done, don't talk about your new plans. Just, don't. And with no news about what you're doing, no hype about what you've done, not even any controversy over whether they should be focusing on you, they're going to get bored and go watch the next Kardashian wedding or Hollywood rehab failure."

Jacob stared at him. "I don't think you get it. We're talking the exposure of my life's biggest horror, the secret I've tried to hide for years. The thing that could keep me out of the Academy."

"And that's a legitimate concern," conceded Daniel. "It's like taking one of the *Toddlers and Tiaras* brats and giving her a patrol car, and I don't see that happening anytime soon. But remember, they're evaluating you, not your television history. And if you're calm and stable while this explodes around you, and you roll through it like a boss, that's going to say a lot more." He tipped his head in the direction of the Con Ops room. "Your friend did you a favor in there, but you can't count on her to save you again."

Jacob looked away. "I don't know that I can just stand there while everyone's watching old clips of me pulling my pants down."

"Well, that might be a challenge." Daniel sighed. "I'm not pretending it'll be easy. I'm just saying that's your best bet, if you want to ride this thing out and look good on the other side."

Jacob propped his head in his hands.

"You and your aunt kept a tight lid on this thing for a long while," Daniel said. "How'd it come out now? Where did all those episodes in the panel rooms come from?"

"I have no idea. But they didn't connect to me, not directly. Not like this." He clenched his fists. "That was Ryan Brazil."

"What?"

"He got wind of the Facebook thing with Sam. Figured I was the one who had reported him, probably since I'd asked him about the pictures. So he checked in my wallet when I had it out on the table, looking for dirt. All he found was the driver's license, but that was enough. And that was his revenge, blowing it up for the entire freaking convention. He gets caught creeping on girls, so I get to lose everything I've worked for over the majority of my life." Jacob shook his head. "Figures he's the kind of low-life who would even watch something like *Cougars and Cold Ones*."

Daniel snorted. "He's a classy fellow, all right. If it helps, just think of him as paying for your college education."

Jacob smiled weakly. "Yeah. Kinda hard to think of him putting me through school."

"You should thank him for it."

Jacob turned to look at Daniel, incredulous.

"No, you should. Right to his face. Let him know that because of him and people like him, you're finishing your degree with no overhanging student loans." Daniel's teeth flashed. "Be very sincere."

Jacob snorted. "Okay, yeah, that might be funny. Right after I get done punching him repeatedly in the face."

Daniel leaned back in his chair. "Sounds like you're going to have to work a bit on that 'ride it out' thing."

They were silent a moment. Jacob sighed and dropped his head into his hands again. His head hurt, and the movement pulled at taut muscles across his neck and shoulders.

"So your aunt Lydia made it," Daniel mused. "She got away from the family sphere and made it into law school. How'd she do it?"

"She worked her freakin' butt off," Jake said.

Daniel raised his eyebrows. "Good for her."

"Yeah. There's a reason she collects superhero figurines. It's like her real family album." Jake grinned tiredly.

"She say that?"

"Nope. Just me. It's true, though. Nobody's tougher than my Aunt Lydia." He tipped his head to one side, stretching his neck.

"What would she do if her connection with the family was exposed?"

Jacob turned an exhausted glare on him. "Now you're cheating." He exhaled. "There isn't a psychological interview for practicing law. It's a lot more academic than profiling."

"Not for clients." Daniel shifted in his chair. "It's personal for clients. Really personal. They need to connect with their attorney, they have to trust her. Right? So what would she do if suddenly that got around, and all her clients and potential clients learned she was part of the *Cougars and Cold Ones* family?"

Jacob picked up an energy drink, turning the can to occupy his hands, and tried to seriously consider it. "She... She would own it. Use it to point out how far she's come, and how it can help her relate to them. We've all got stuff we need to get past, and she's gotten past hers, and let her help you past yours." He paused. "I hadn't thought about it, but yeah, that's what she'd do. Own it."

"Hm." Daniel nodded once. "Smart lady, your aunt."

Jacob didn't answer.

A moment passed, and then Daniel stood. "Okay, let's get back to Ops and see what else is on fire now. And oh, how I hope that's not literal."

Chapter Twenty Eight

Daniel's encouragement made Jacob feel a little better, until they reached the lobby and he saw a hotel screen and the rotating *Happy Birthday Little Jakey Tarston* message.

His steps slowed, and Daniel gave him an understanding look. "I'll go ask the front desk to take it down," he said.

Jacob nodded, and the officer walked away.

This was it. Everything he'd tried to leave behind, to bury, had come to threaten what he had and nearly had. If Daniel was right, if there was some chance he could survive this thing, he could afford no misstep at this moment. Stay focused, move forward, ride it out.

Someone who wanted to get into police work for the right reasons, who wouldn't endanger or embarrass the department? That façade of normality was pretty much blown out of the water now. He wanted to do the work — but now he would have to prove he was capable.

And he had a chance to do so right now. He was in the center of a multiple-homicide investigation which had stymied the force thus far. If he found the killer now, they would have to recognize his potential. No, not potential, not after that — his skill.

He'd worked toward this for years, taken specialized classes and trained physically all with the goal of entering the Academy and eventually making Detective. He wasn't going to lose that, wasn't going to let it be taken from him by a single cruel prank at a gathering of what was supposed to be like-minded enthusiasts and friends.

"It's gone," Daniel said, returning. "I'm going to bed. Again. You going to be okay?"

Jacob nodded. "Nothing rash, I promise."

"Good. Hang in there, give me an update tomorrow morning." Daniel headed for the elevators.

Jacob took the folded sheet with his mind map from his pocket and spread it flat. He had notes, he had local insight. One of Jessica's classic mystery sleuths would have said he had everything he needed to uncover the killer. Now he just had to do it.

And it would be a helluva lot easier on his mind than thinking of everyone staring up at the *Cougars and Cold Ones* screen.

He threw himself into a chair and stared at the mind map. The scarcity of lines connecting events and facts mocked him. He knew nothing.

A man in hotel livery was fumbling with the pass-through's security grate; the staff was tired, too. Jacob saw Paul leaving the Con Ops room. "Are we locking up?"

"Yeah," Paul said. "Vince wanted someone here all night, but I'm done. It's been a long and crazy day, as if you didn't know, and I'm toast."

Jacob nodded. "I hear ya." He glanced at the energy drink in his hand and then held it up. "I'm not going to bed anytime soon. You want me to cover the graveyard shift?"

"Would you?" Paul looked grateful. "I can't imagine there would be much, just if the overnight panels or viewing rooms had a problem. Anything major, drunks at the dance or something, you can call hotel security. Thanks, thanks a lot. I know you've gone way beyond the call of duty this weekend."

"Not a problem." Jacob gave him a little salute. "I'm not exactly in a sleeping mood." And staying overnight would let him browse the computer and the submitted photos.

The hotel employee put the grate back up. "If you decide to close up," he said, "have the front desk call maintenance, and they'll get someone here with a key."

"Got it." Jacob settled himself again into the chair and took a drink. It had been a long day, but maybe the caffeine would kick his brain into a higher gear. Surely there would be a clue in the photos, something to suggest the killer or even just the motive.

He turned to the computer and alt-tabbed to the Twitter feed. Time to scan.

Several hundred con-goers had tweeted pictures of the conservatory and lobby, and Jacob downloaded each of the hashtagged photos into a folder. The police would be gathering the photos submitted through Flickr, and those probably wouldn't be shared, but he could browse the Twitter photos with the #ConJobPhotoReq hashtag.

For any clues. He felt like such an idiot, working outside the official investigation and not even as a proper investigator. Despite the pink- and green-clad costumed characters with their plush Great Dane in the hall, meddling kids didn't solve real crimes while the police bumbled through comedy. But Jacob's secret was out, and he was never going to be a proper investigator in an official investigation if he didn't somehow prove that he was capable despite his humiliating background.

There were hundreds of pictures of group photoshoots in the conservatory, often a dozen or more of nearly the identical shot. *Star Trek, My Little Ponies, Naruto, Doctor Who,* Batman and assorted villains and colleagues, *Supernatural, Game of Thrones, Sherlock, Avengers* and friends....

Jacob sighed. The photos were mostly obligatory line-ups, group hugs, mock battles, shipping of paired characters or the occasional threesome, and other pictures which seemed to have nothing at all to do with any of the three murders. This was a waste of time and computer memory.

Others had tweeted photos they'd taken of individual cosplayers or small groups. Here was a complete crew of the *Serenity,* here were just Wash and Zoë with their arms comfortably about one another, and then another picture of Wash crouching wide-eyed behind Zoë as she brandished an enormous gun. Here was a picture of Darth Vader force-choking a Mandalorian. Here was Pyramid Head threatening a Nurse. Here was one of Sailor Moon with Sailors Mercury, Venus, Mars, Jupiter, Saturn, Neptune, and Uranus, with Sailor Pluto off a few steps sobbing into her hands. Jacob smiled at that one.

There were photos of the zombie apocalypse now, too, even though no request had actually gone out yet. It was good to know that people wanted to be helpful, but it meant several hundred more photos to sort through, most of which didn't include the zombie victim. Jacob decided to skip them for the moment and concentrate on what Laser might have inadvertently captured in the conservatory.

He found more photos of *Supernatural* and *Once Upon A Time* characters, Sherlock, John Watson, and Mycroft all facing down a defiant Moriarty, a large gold ballgown resembling a Dalek and a large blue one clearly meant to represent the

TARDIS. And then there was a photo of the CLUTCH cosplayer, all white and flowing silks, before her grey-green encounter with the Mole. She was kneeling, one arm outstretched to display the embroidery. The photo's edge showed a shoulder and arm which probably belonged to Laser, so the photo had been shot alongside her as she was working. It was a different angle than Laser's, as she would not have set up a shot to include the service door which broke up the beautiful conservatory background, even half-hidden behind a potted topiary.

The user had tweeted several photos, taken in sequence, of the gorgeous costume. The second showed the service door half open, with a figure coming through. The figure's face and torso were shielded by the door. More of Laser was visible in this photo as well, looking down at the settings on her camera.

The third photo was blurred, and Jacob couldn't see much more than Laser holding her camera with one hand and pointing across the frame, probably at someone holding an off-camera flash. Jacob had seen enough of her shoots, some of Sam, to imagine that she was calling instructions to change the angle of the flash or adjust the speed.

The fourth photo showed Laser slightly out of focus, still calling instructions to her flash assistant. The cosplayer was also out of focus, not selected by the camera's auto-focus. The service door was more fully open, showing a second man entering behind the first, not really visible. The second was in some sort of *sentai* costume. The first could now be seen more clearly, dressed in the red and orange uniform of the Fierce Burger franchise. He was in front of the door, captured mid-stride past the topiary, and he was looking straight at Laser.

Jacob stopped and looked at the photo, just staring. It meant nothing, really. Anyone might have stopped to look at the photographer crouching in the middle of the floor and calling instructions. The fact that a fast food worker was curious about the photographer meant nothing.

Why was a fast food worker coming out of the service corridor? The conservatory didn't link to the food court, where the Fierce Burger counter was. Again, it meant nothing on its own, but he was curious.

Jacob looked at the second man, but the door obscured too much. It might have been the Terra Vista Ranger, but there was no shortage of *sentai* sources, and even if it were it could have been either Christopher Adams or someone doing a version in homage of the Big Name Fan, which happened occasionally.

He moused down to the zoom selection and blew up the picture, but it didn't help much. The first man was clearly looking right at Laser, pixelated eyes right on her.

Jacob made a note of the file name. The police would see them all eventually, but it would be good to point this one out first. Laser hadn't been a murder victim, but it would be good to find her assailant as well.

He moved back to the filtered tweets with hashtags and found the next photo. And he realized his efforts on the previous one had been superfluous, because this was the photo they needed.

The photo was another of the CLUTCH cosplayer, who filled most of the frame. But the inexpert photographer had caught Laser at the side of the photo, still looking at her off-camera assistant. Her camera was pointing off as she gestured elsewhere, and Jacob knew from watching Sam's shoots that she was firing disposable photos as she tested the flashes. The camera was angled toward the service door, and while Laser wasn't even looking in that direction, it was likely she had captured a couple of photos of it.

At the door, the Fierce Burger employee had turned back in apparent protest. The second man's eyes were fixed on Laser, dark and hard. And his face, caught in the camera's auto-focus, was sharp enough to identify as Christopher Adams.

Chapter Twenty Nine

It probably meant nothing. It certainly proved nothing. Laser, and at least one other con attendee, had photographed Christopher Adams in the background during the photoshoot of Achenar from *Crooked Running Water* by CLUTCH, the Heavenly Wedding arc, artbook version.

There were a hundred reasons why Christopher might be looking directly at Laser, ranging from the fact that she was crouching on the open floor and making noise to the fact that she was calling instructions to the fact that she was a pretty girl who might draw a man's eyes. None of that suggested any acts of violence.

There were probably perfectly good reasons why Christopher might be emerging from a service corridor as well. Laser herself had said that she liked to shoot some costumes in such places for the claustrophobic atmosphere. And Christopher was wearing his trademark Terra Vista Ranger costume, so he might have been working with another photographer. Jacob could ask him. It seemed unlikely, anyway, that he would have been doing a photoshoot with the Fierce Burger employee.

Maybe the Fierce Burger guy wasn't really a Fierce Burger employee, or at least wasn't from the conference food court. Jacob might have missed an advertising campaign which had become a sort of meme or gained an underground following. Stranger things had happened, and Jacob had seen cosplayers of insurance spokespeople, fast food mascots, and even retail products themselves.

The Fierce Burger guy didn't seem to be simply holding the door for Christopher but was looking directly at him. Jacob squinted. Was he gesturing at Laser? It was hard to say. But he had been looking at her in the previous photo, so perhaps he was.

Jacob enlarged each of the photos, scrolling and adjusting the frames so that he could look at just the two men, both photos displayed side by side. Christopher looked serious, far more intense than a shortcut through a service corridor should warrant. And the Fierce Burger worker also looked serious and a bit alarmed.

Jacob studied the first photo, in which the fast food worker faced the camera. The employee in the red and orange shirt looked vaguely familiar, though Jacob couldn't place him. He hadn't eaten at the Fierce Burger, so perhaps that meant he was a cosplayer?

The police would determine if the photos were further reason to interview Christopher again. Jacob made a note of the filename and saved the second picture as well.

The man in the Fierce Burger shirt.... His face nagged at Jacob. Surely there was something significant about him. Was he another BNF?

After a moment, Jacob alt-tabbed back to the Twitter window. He considered a moment, and then typed and edited to fit the character limit. *Does anyone have photos of the Fierce Burger guy in conservatory? Behind Achenar. (This is not an official police request.) #ConJobPhotoReq*

The parenthetical disclaimer should keep him out of trouble, and should keep the fast food worker out of trouble too by emphasizing that he wasn't a police suspect. Jacob wasn't wholly sure of the legal niceties, but he hoped that was enough to protect anyone. But maybe another photo or two would jog his Fierce Burger memory.

He leaned back and stretched, and then he rubbed his eyes. They burned, dry with indoor air and stress. It had been a long, long day, and he should feel sleepy — but it was difficult to feel sleepy after the mortally-wounded zombie had slumped in his arms.

Music started playing in the lobby down the corridor, a theme from a classic video game Jacob couldn't quite remember. The Spork Minstrels were playing another set. Jacob closed his eyes and listened through the end of the song, when a scattering of applause indicated the remaining group of con attendees still in the lobby area.

You can do this, Jacob. You have knowledge-local. Lydia's words echoed through his mind. Jacob wasn't so sure. If witnesses had reported a figure in red and blue Spandex fleeing from a falling corpse, he could use his comics knowledge and con savvy to narrow down the list of possible characters and then what groups might contain such a cosplayer. But this was beyond his con attendee abilities. This was a police investigation, not a geek endeavor.

He propped his face in his hands, letting his fingers cool his aching eyes. He thought of Jessica, rolling her eyes and breathing out irate indignation over inane rants about fake geek girls. Jacob wondered if he might now qualify as something like that himself: *Fake geek sleuth. Fake Academy potential.*

"Don't crash yet, man. Sunday's not over."

Jacob withdrew his hands and looked at Sergio, leaning over the pass-through. "Can you give me a nudge when it's safe to wake up?"

"Hang in there. Drink some Red Bull or Monster."

Jacob shook his head. "What do you want?"

Sergio came in the door. "First of all, I found these, and they seem like the kind of thing someone would want back." He set two off-camera flashes on the table.

"Oh, wow," Jacob said. "Yeah, everyone's been looking for those. Where were they?"

"Men's restroom, the back one way behind Main that no one uses. They were in the trash can under some paper towels, but it's a short can and they showed a little bit."

"Thanks. Definitely wanted these. They're probably Laser's." He folded them into a spare Con Aid t-shirt and tucked them into a bin. Sergio had probably unknowingly compromised the fingerprints, but there still might be some recoverable evidence.

"No kidding? Somebody stole Laser's flashes?"

"Somebody assaulted her and stole some equipment."

"Laser got hurt?"

"She's okay, just got banged up a little. But yeah, someone knocked her down and stole her gear bag. That's why we were asking for pictures, wondering if maybe somebody was afraid of a photo she took."

Sergio whistled. "Poor Laser. So it wasn't just theft?"

"It could have been, if the thief's stupid. Which is always possible. But it looked like he'd taken the camera and SD cards and some cheaper stuff, left some of the really expensive gear he could have resold. And now it looks like he ditched the flashes. So that implies some other purpose than resale — or, as we said, a stupid criminal."

"I guess if he had brains or marketable skills, he wouldn't be a criminal." Sergio shrugged. "Well, maybe. Maybe he just got unlucky." He hesitated. "Hey, about my money… I remember what you said about never ever spend what you don't have, and you sounded pretty serious about that. And you said I should talk to my credit card company before it's due, maybe work something out, and I thought maybe were you talking from experience, and I thought maybe you could tell me what kind of thing I could work out?"

Jacob stared at him. "Seriously? It's, what, two am, and you're asking me about negotiating your credit card debt?"

Sergio looked surprised. "You're up anyway."

Jacob sighed. "I wasn't talking from that kind of experience, at least not like you're thinking. But you should talk to them, yeah. They'd rather negotiate with you and get something than have you default and get nothing, and bill collectors are not as profitable as you just paying. It won't be easy for you, and it probably won't look great on your record, but it'll look better than having some crazy debt hanging over your head forever."

"So I can work something out? Pay it off a little at a time, at a reasonable interest?"

"I don't know about reasonable, but it'll probably be better than what you'll pay on the card agreement. Or maybe you can borrow somewhere at a lower rate to pay off the card. Point is, do something in advance, or you're going to hurt when that bill comes and interest starts stacking up."

"Okay. I'll call them on Monday."

Jacob yawned. "See, not urgent. Could have waited."

"What? I had to drop off the flashes. And I wasn't going to sleep. Rough weekend, finding out Rick got burned and I'm getting stiffed."

"It's been a rough weekend for everybody. A lot of the con attendees are getting off pretty easy, nothing but the chaos about the food, but the hotel staff is getting pounded, the con staff are of course going crazy, and the police can't take a break without another body showing up. Even the food court staff got burned, getting shut down for the weekend. That's a lot of work they don't have."

"Yeah, I feel bad for the food court people. Bet the employees were expecting a lot of hours this weekend."

Sergio would be feeling particularly sensitive to the plight of expecting money which wasn't coming, after all. "Yeah, I don't know what company policy would be on that. Not sure if the handbook has something on service suspended because of suspected poisonings."

"Some of 'em might have been okay with it, though. I knew some were waiting to get off so they could do the con, too, and I guess this just gave them more con time."

"I guess statistically some of them would have to be fans."

"Yeah. A burger guy yesterday was going to do the zombie crawl, was all excited about it. They had to make up fresh fries, and while I was waiting he told me all about his costume and the special makeup he had planned and everything."

Something shifted sickeningly in Jacob's mind. "Burger guy? Where?" He hoped his voice sounded casual.

"Oh, um, Fierce Burger. Yeah. I ate there last night. The fries are really good, worth waiting for even though they're always running out."

Jacob's thoughts froze up for a moment. Was the Fierce Burger employee familiar because Jacob had met him at the zombie crawl? Was the memory unclear because his face had been obscured beneath the prosthetics and makeup? Jacob had a shiver of guilt that he couldn't be certain of the young man who had practically died in his arms.

And if it were the murdered zombie, then that added another layer of suspicion to the picture of Laser's photoshoot.

He had been looking hard at Laser, and someone had attacked her.

"Do you think you could recognize the guy?" he asked.

Sergio looked at him. "Huh? I dunno, why?"

Jacob opened the photos and selected just the Fierce Burger employee's face, cutting out the rest of the photo. "This. Can you tell me if it's him?"

Sergio leaned toward the computer. "Maybe. I don't know, I was just getting dinner, not really paying attention to people. But — yeah, I think it's him. He had that big zit on the side of his nose, you can sort of see it there. Kind of nasty in a food service job, but what can you do?"

"So that's him?"

"I think so."

What if some vigilante type had learned it was the Fierce Burger zombie who had assaulted Laser, and so he had killed him in return? Laser was popular, she had a lot of fans. But no, vigilantism didn't seem right, not when police were already on the scene and clearly taking the incident seriously — and investigating other deaths, making vigilante action even riskier than usual. Perhaps the murderer had hired the Fierce Burger zombie to rob Laser, so he could get the unknown evidence while establishing an alibi himself elsewhere.

Sergio was still looking at him expectantly. "Why? Is he the con killer?"

Jacob stared at him. "Does he have a nickname now?"

"It's an easy phrase, nice and alliterative. Con killer. There's a few tweets going around with that hashtag, offering girls escort services to their rooms, with both noble and prurient motivations."

Jacob shook his head. "Oh, Jessica will have something to say about that, that's for sure."

"So, do you think it's him?"

"What? No. No, I don't."

"But you wanted to know about him."

"Because I have a picture of a Fierce Burger guy at a conservatory photoshoot, which seemed kind of weird. But that's not any kind of illegal, or threatening, or anything else, and it makes perfectly decent sense if he's a fan." Jacob wrinkled his face. "If you thought his zit was nasty, you should just be glad he wasn't in decomposing zombie makeup or anything while he was working."

"Now that is disgusting."

"Yeah, it is." Jacob withdrew his phone and wrote a text to Daniel. *Hey, I know you're asleep right now, but when you get this, can you check and see if the zombie victim was a Fierce Burger employee?*

Sergio was still looking at him oddly, and Jacob thought he was probably still wondering about Jacob's suspicion. "No, I really don't think he's a suspect. Actually, if you can keep it quiet, I think he might have been someone who got hurt. I don't know that they have an ID on the guy who was killed last night."

"Oh, the guy who had his throat cut at the zombie crawl?" Sergio's mouth twisted. "That had to be rough, man. I wasn't there, but from what I heard…. It'd be like some sort of nightmare, trying to get someone to help and everyone's just laughing at your zany zombie antics. That's true horror, man."

"No argument there." Jacob's voice was sober. "We were even getting a little angry that he was leaving blood smears. It was Sam who realized it was real blood. I wish… I wish there was some way to apologize."

"Who do you think killed him? Same guy who killed the other two?"

"I don't know. That's a pretty big jump in method, from poison to slashing a throat, and especially with the victim out and visible in a crowd. That's not vanilla murder, that's psycho look-at-me stuff."

"I guess you learn that stuff in cop class."

"Still just an undergrad. Hoping to be in real cop class soon."

"So we're looking at two murderers? Or three?"

"Well, there's a chance that the murdered zombie wasn't turned loose to die in the crawl. Apparently the medical people think he lasted a pretty long time for the type of injury, so maybe the murderer didn't expect him to get out and look for help at all. That would take it to slightly less psycho, anyway. But it's still a big jump in method, so something would have had to push him pretty hard, so maybe it is two people. And then there's the guy who attacked Laser, so...."

"So we've either got a couple of murderers and a violent mugger loose, if we're unlucky, or if we're lucky just one really crazy and unpredictable SOB. That doesn't actually make me feel any better." Sergio shook his head. "And on that delightful note, I'm going to head over and see if there's any cup ramen left at the food tables. Thanks for the credit card tip."

Chapter Thirty

Jacob drummed his fingers on the desktop and stared at the screen. Something hovered about the edge of his mind, teasing him with its feathery nearness, but he couldn't quite grasp it. Frustrated, he pushed the chair back and picked up the sheet of printer paper he'd been doodling on — oh, only hours ago, when Daniel had brought the shoplifter in. It seemed like days.

The two circles in the middle of the page — *why kill Tasha/Dead-Laura?* And *why kill Valerie K?* — were insufficient now. He added, *why kill zombie/possible Fierce Burger guy?*

Off to one side, he tried to add, *why attack Laser and steal equipment?* But the writing was cramped and bent along the edge of the paper. And when he started to add a note about finding the flashes but not the SD cards, he realized he was going to need a bigger sheet. He thought best when doodling and writing out snippets of thought, but his handwriting, as Lydia teased, was best suited to keyboards. He needed more room.

He turned to the over-sized easel in the corner, waiting for updates to staff schedules, photo gatherings, police interviews, whatever needed to be posted on the Con Ops wall. Jacob shook out the little box of markers on the tray and flipped to a clean sheet.

Red for murders, right in the middle. *Tasha/Dead-Laura* on the left, *Valerie K* in the center, *zombie/Fierce Burger guy?* on the right. A little beneath them, floating somewhere between

Valerie and zombie/Fierce Burger, he wrote Laser's name with a question mark. She hadn't been murdered, certainly, but it had been a violent assault which could have gone much worse, and the attack might be connected to the deaths.

He took up the blue marker and began to list all the incidents which were probably connected to the crimes. *Powder in kitchen. Photography gear abandoned. Missing camera and SD cards. R-F-T or R-V-D killed zombie/Fierce Burger guy.*

Orange marker next, for all the weird things which might or might not be connected. *CaCO in viewing rooms, panels, vendor hall. S out $8k. RB creeping on girls. Con in debt. VC took money.*

Green marker for all the things which weren't necessarily odd or out of place, but were definitely present and influential. *Photos and photobombs. RB outs CaCO. Cosplay. Voice acting. Theft in vendor hall. Viewing rooms. Dance.*

Just as he had done on the printer sheet, he drew a dotted line between *photos and photobombs* and *Laser.* He drew another to connect them with *missing camera and SD cards.* He linked Tasha and Valerie, with another dotted line to indicate an uncertain connection with the white powder found in the kitchen.

He thought a moment and then wrote in, *Access to kitchens* and connected it to the zombie/Fierce Burger circle. Maybe the zombie had poisoned the two women, and someone had learned and retaliated instead of going to police. That would explain the difference in methods and approach. Poison was calculated and planned, while punching and knifing were more likely to be done in anger, a moment of fury.

"You're still here?"

Jacob whirled, startled, and then felt foolish. "Oh, hi. Yeah." He capped the marker and gave a sheepish grin to

Christopher Adams, who was leaning upon the pass-through. "Holding the fort in the graveyard shift. And mixing my metaphors, I guess."

"I hope you've at least got something to drink back there."

"I don't like to drink alone." Jacob shrugged. "Too young to start that downward spiral." He smiled and wondered if he should ask about the service corridor and the Fierce Burger employee.

Christopher was wearing his Terra Vista Ranger costume. He reached down to a backpack he was carrying and brought up a metal flask with a screen-printed logo of himself as Terra Vista Ranger on it. "Well, if I came in, you wouldn't be alone."

"Can't argue with that logic." Jacob dropped the marker onto the easel tray. Normally he wasn't a big drinker; he'd watched far too much of its effects growing up to want to risk losing any of his own self-control and independence. But there was a lot of social pressure on students to drink, and he'd finally started drinking a little just to make the comments stop.

Christopher came inside and let the door swing closed again with a faint little click. "You don't mind sharing, do you?"

Jacob started for the other side of the room. "Um, I'm pretty sure there's some paper cups or something around here, left over. I'm fighting a cold or something, you probably don't want to share with me."

Sharing meant taking a drink each time it was passed or faking a drink. And besides the risk of being caught faking, faking a drink always felt really awkward, like he was lying to the people around him, and then he'd wonder if he should care about lying to people who had already pressured him into doing something he didn't really want to do, and maybe he *should* be lying to them just to assert himself, or maybe be more assertive about not drinking in the first place, and then he'd start to think he'd been listening to Jessica too much. It was much easier to nurse a cup of his own and let other people lose track of his progress.

He found a stack of plastic cups in a box beneath a table and turned back to Christopher, who was studying the easel. "Is this how the investigation's going?" he asked, taking a sip from his flask.

"Sort of," Jacob said. "That's not official, just — er, I was just mind-mapping." Was there anything on there that shouldn't be seen? He started back toward the easel.

"Does that work?" came a third voice.

It was Mickey Groene, waving from the pass-through. "Sorry, was just passing by. But now that I see the price of admission, do you mind if I join you?" He held up a six-pack of dark bottles.

"Come on in," Christopher said cheerily. "We can share, and — Jacob? — Jacob can tell us how he's solving the murder."

"Oh." Mickey sobered a little as he entered and closed the door again. "Any leads?"

Jacob shook his head and gestured to the easel. "No, like I was saying, that's just my own scribbles."

"And I was asking if it worked."

"It helps me organize my head." He held out three cups to distract them. "Something has to." He smiled.

Christopher smiled too, and he reached to pour a couple inches of amber liquid into two of the cups. "You a private eye or something?"

Jacob laughed. "Not quite. I'm finishing up police

science in school, and I'm applying to the Academy soon. So I'm just a wannabe."

Christopher laughed. "That's a lousy thing to say about anyone. You're not a wannabe."

"Yeah, I'll hold off on that until after I'm officially accepted, thanks." Maybe Christopher hadn't seen the Jakey Tarston screens.

Mickey nodded toward the easel. "Well, this looks pretty complicated."

"Not really." Jacob pointed out the circles, partially blocking the paper. He wasn't really comfortable sharing this, especially with Christopher in those photos. He would play it cool and then put it away for drinks, leaving them less curious than if he hastily hid it. "This is all the stuff that's been going on, and this stuff is probably connected, but we haven't — that is, I haven't put all the pieces together yet. I can't speak for the official investigation, obviously."

"They don't keep you in the loop?"

"That'd be like a chemistry major getting to sit in on a FDA hearing. Nope, they don't have to tell me anything except whether I'm free to go." Jacob laughed.

"But you're also con staff," Christopher said, "and since this is clearly something to do with Con Job, you should be entitled to some sort of update."

"I'm not staff, just a volunteer. And no, they still don't have to tell me anything, even if I were. Even Vince is in the dark with the rest of us."

"Poor Vince. This must be hitting him hard." Christopher took a drink.

"I can't even imagine," Mickey agreed.

Jacob wondered if this were Christopher's way of fishing for information. Maybe word of the sticky financial situation had gotten around. "Yeah, he's been pretty upset about it. They even wanted to question him — but hey, we're all suspects, right?"

"We are?"

"Pretty much everyone in the building, sort of, but of course no one's arresting people just for that. It's just that, this looks almost random. So that makes it harder to sort out suspects."

"Random, like some sort of psychopath?"

"Whoa, don't start talking that way, people will go nuts. And it's probably not accurate, anyway, even leaving aside the fact that 'psychopath' is a pretty broad and nontechnical term. It's just that there's nothing obviously connecting the murders, you know? So it looks random."

"But you don't think so."

"It's not about what I think, it's just a matter of probabilities. You're not going to get three random murders, two with the same method, in the same hotel in the same weekend." He shrugged and grinned. "And well, yeah, I don't think so."

Christopher leaned forward and refilled Jacob's cup, though it hadn't gone down much. He took his own drink straight from the flask, and Jacob was momentarily grateful for the antiseptic qualities of alcohol. "You're right," Christopher said. "Those first two deaths were the same, weren't they?"

"Were they?" asked Mickey.

They looked at Jacob, and suddenly he couldn't remember if the causes of death had been publicly announced. But yes, they had, because people knew why the kitchens were being cleared. "Yeah," he said. "But the third was different. Everyone saw the guy bleeding in the hallway. That was horrible, and I hope they find the guy."

"How do you know it's a guy?" asked Mickey.

"Statistically more likely," Jacob said. "The victim was hit in the face and his throat was cut. Women certainly can do stuff like that, but it's a more typically male approach."

Mickey went over to look at the easel, deflating Jacob's hopes that they would move on. "So what's all this?"

Jacob stood, uneasy. "Um, I'm not sure you guys should be looking at that."

"You just said you weren't a cop yet, and that they didn't tell you all the updates. So anything you know should be okay for us, right?" Christopher spun in his chair to look at the mind map.

Jacob started forward, but Mickey was already pointing at a circle. "RB creeping on girls? Is that—"

"That's not common knowledge," Jacob said hurriedly, "and it's not related to the homicide investigations, and I'm pretty sure I shouldn't be talking about it. Sorry."

"What about this cocoa thing?" Christopher asked, pointing at the *CaCO* notation.

Jacob's ears grew warm and he knew he was blushing. He hoped the others would miss it in the mediocre lighting. "That's not related to the homicide investigations, either."

"Oh, I saw that on the screens and Twitter," Mickey said.

The heat spread from Jacob's ears to his face and neck. "I'm never gonna get away from it now."

Mickey stepped nearer and clapped him on the shoulder. "Don't be such a teenager. Of course you will; you've got all kinds of time in front of you. And trust me, I know what I'm talking about. I was pretty sure I'd never work again after *Posy Picnic Massacre*. I fired my agent and I spent the week after release hiding in my apartment, drinking cheap beer and eating canned refried beans because I was too scared to go to the grocery where someone might recognize me." He smiled a crooked little smile. "But after a couple of months, the internet moved on to something else shiny, and I got another job. Which just happened to be *Death Walks Quietly*, and that was a huge break for me."

Jacob sighed and nodded. It was too hard to argue it again.

Christopher seemed to take pity on him and tried to change the subject. "What's the RVD thing?"

"Oh, that's actually pretty sad." Jacob nodded toward the easel. "The zombie — I'm sorry, that's kind of a terrible thing to call him. But the guy who died after the zombie crawl, who was made up like a zombie, he told us that right before the EMTs came. That's who attacked him, who actually killed him."

Christopher blinked. "He talked? In initials? That's like some crazy movie script."

"No, he was whispering, and that's what we could make out. Those are consonants in the murderer's name."

Christopher swore. "That's freaky. And scary. Who's got initials like that? Rupert Vincent Dare? No, that sounds like an adventure comic. Wait, did they — did they talk to Vince?"

"Does it have to be either of those two sets?" Mickey asked. "Because if you were just grabbing consonants, then it seems like they could be in any arrangement, right?"

"Well, they have to be in that order." Jacob was confused.

"Yeah, but not necessarily in that grouping. So you've got RVD and RFT, but it could also be RFD and RVT. Right?"

Jacob considered. "Oh, yeah, right." He reached for a marker to write them in.

"No, blue," Mickey corrected, handing him the right color. "I don't know what all the colors mean, but obviously they matter."

"It's not a very good system," Jacob said. He wrote in the extra visemes and frowned at the paper. *Blue....*

"Good thing I'm the Terra Vista Ranger, and not the Ranger Vista Terra. That would be awkward." Christopher frowned. "What happens if those initials get out and people start going crazy looking for matches? That could get ugly."

"They're not out," Jacob said. "And don't say anything about them, please. I wouldn't even know them except I'm the one who asked the guy."

Mickey's expression softened. "That must have been terrible."

"Yeah, it's pretty bad. A dying statement can be admitted in court only if you ask the victim if he knows he's dying. There's no way for it not to be rough."

"Ouch. Man."

"It can be used in court even if the victim himself is no longer alive to testify?" asked Christopher.

"It's the only time hearsay evidence can be admitted. The theory is, someone who knows he's dying has no reason to lie."

"But only the guy who heard it, or else it's just hearsay again."

"Right."

"Weird. I'd never heard of that." Christopher took another drink. "So who was he? The dying statement victim?"

"We haven't heard yet," Jacob said.

"You wrote here that he's a Fierce Burger employee."

"I don't actually know that, it's just my hunch at the moment." Jacob thought of the conservatory photos. "Actually, do you know a Fierce Burger guy?"

"What? I mean, I eat there, but I don't know if I know anyone who works there...." Christopher's mouth twisted. "Well, maybe. I mean, I don't know."

Mickey frowned at him. "It's not a hard question."

Christopher turned. "It's a hard question if a burger employee has just been murdered and you don't want to accidentally implicate yourself."

"Sorry, man." Mickey held up his hands in appeasement. "Don't get snippy about it. We're all in this together, wanting this guy caught."

"Anyway, yeah, I talked to a Fierce Burger guy for a while, but it's not like we're friends or anything." Christopher took another drink. "Sorry. It's just — this has been a really freaky weekend."

"Ain't that the truth." Mickey held out his cup for a refill.

They were silent for a while, but it wasn't a comfortable silence. Jacob wondered how to ask what Christopher and the Fierce Burger employee had talked about without sounding suspicious.

Mickey stared at the easel and Jacob's mind map. "Red seems kind of brutal," he said after a while. "I mean, yeah, maybe the most important, but a bit brutal."

"Huh?" Jacob followed his eyes to the easel.

"In the middle, the victims' names, in red. Just kinda, you know, hurts to look at them."

"I wasn't thinking that hard about it. I mean, I was using different colors, but they didn't have any particular color meaning other than different layers."

"They should be, I don't know, green or blue or something."

Blue.... The feathery whisper brushed against Jacob's

mind again, like a finger tracing his skin, and he grasped after it. But Mickey was still talking, and it slipped away.

"Or maybe not green, because that's all about life and growing and — sorry, my girlfriend's big into color symbolism. Uses it in all her work, though I don't think most people get what she's thinking. Maybe it still works subconsciously, I don't know. Don't tell her I said that, though." He smiled faintly. "You and Sam, are you…?"

Jacob shook his head. "Just friends."

"Bitch," said Christopher.

Jacob's head jerked toward him. "What?"

"Friend-zoned," Christopher said. "Sorry, man."

Jacob couldn't formulate a coherent reply. "I'm not — she didn't friend-zone me. We're just friends."

"Oh. I didn't realize — I didn't know you were gay. Sorry."

Jacob stared at him, and Mickey cut in. "You got a girlfriend, Christopher?"

"Used to." Christopher took another drink from his flask.

Mickey traded glances with Jacob. Well, that explained it.

Christopher drew out his phone and began to scroll. "Looks like you're getting a lot of photos coming in."

"Yeah, people have been sending hundreds. A few fakes — seriously, who pranks a homicide investigation? — but mostly legit."

"Anything useful?"

"Well, that's hard to say. There's a reason these things usually take a long time to investigate."

Christopher held up his phone. "There's a request for pictures of the Fierce Burger guy. You said that was just your theory."

"Yeah, I tweeted that. Hope I don't get in trouble for it. But he looks kind of like the zombie who was killed, if you try to look past all the makeup and special effects."

"Huh. And you got photos of him in the conservatory?"

"I haven't checked yet. Do you see anything new?" Jacob turned to the computer on the desk, wondering if Christopher would mention again his contact with the employee.

"Nothing yet. Why the conservatory?"

Christopher might be afraid of association; a lot of people did that, didn't volunteer information because they thought it might make them a suspect. He could be feeling Jacob out to know whether it was safe to mention that he'd been there, too. Or he might not be mentioning it because he had something more significant to hide. "Um, I saw a photo of him there. In the background of another shot. I thought someone else's photo might show more of what he was doing there."

Christopher shrugged. "A guy can walk through a hotel public space, right?"

"Yeah, but in the photo, he was looking kind of funny at Laser — from Laser Focus Photography, you know her? And a little later she was assaulted and robbed."

Mickey swore. "Is she okay?"

"Yeah, she's okay. Scary, though."

"Obviously."

"So you think he did it?" asked Christopher.

"I don't think anything solid yet," Jacob said. "And I'm just a wannabe detective killing time in the middle of the night with theories."

Christopher took another drink. "I think you're selling

yourself short," he said. "I think you've got a lot more you're working with."

"Oh?"

"All those photos you've been looking at on Twitter," Christopher said, "I've been looking at them, too. Everyone can see them, following the hashtag. So you already know that I was in the photo with the Fierce Burger guy."

Jacob's pulse quickened. "Well, yeah, but it wasn't really clear. And I didn't want to sound like I was saying anything about you."

"Why not?" Christopher turned to look hard at him. "Because you were worried about my reputation?"

"Well, no, there's no one here to talk about your reputation," Jacob said awkwardly. "I was just being polite."

"Just being polite," Christopher repeated, "or you were just keeping your mouth shut because you were suspicious of me."

Jacob held up his hands. "Calm down, man. It's just a picture of you and a guy together. There's probably a couple hundred pictures of people with that guy just on his Facebook page. It doesn't mean anything on its own."

"But you thought it meant something, or you wouldn't have tweeted about more photos."

"Hey," Mickey said, "go easy, Christopher. You're kind of over-reacting to this."

"Shut up, Mickey."

Mickey's face darkened but his voice remained steady. "There's no call to be this way. It's been a hard weekend on everybody, but we don't want to leave with nasty impressions of each other. People are stressed, but when we get back to —"

"Get back to what? I've got nothing to go back to. You've got a bunch of shows and games and I don't know, commercials and whatever. I've got no show at all, thanks to that freakin' bitch and her bitch sister."

Mickey stiffened, and Jacob remembered his clandestine relationship. Jacob glanced at Mickey, but the voice actor gave a minute shake of his head, without looking at Jacob.

Christopher's jaw clenched. "I thought for a bit that maybe now that she's dead, maybe the rest of MEGAN!ME would pick up the show again."

Jacob made a show of pushing the alcohol away from him. "Time to slow down, I think."

"We all think privately of how things will change when something happens to someone and whether or not we'll get called as a result," Mickey said quietly. "Like I got brought in once when Rob Paulsen got strep throat. Just, most of us have the decency to keep it to ourselves."

"Yeah, but you got called in for Rob freaking Paulsen! He's a legend. I just need to get paid for the show I was promised." Christopher gestured sharply. "Is that so much to ask? Just get paid for my work? But no, some tarted-up slut in a powersuit decides to cut me for a *chibi* mascot to nepotism, and I'm out of luck."

Mickey frowned. "Are you saying Valerie dropped your show idea because she wanted to use a *chibi*?"

Jacob stopped listening, because Christopher's rant had finally anchored the drifting, nagging thought in his head. *Blue.*

Girls noticed these things, right? He pulled out his phone and texted Sam, wondering if she were still awake. *What was MEGAN!ME Valerie wearing when we saw her? Be specific if you can.*

Mickey and Christopher were still arguing about the *chibi* character. Jacob rotated in his chair and opened Google on the computer. It was easy to find: Shadow's wife Laura was buried in a blue suit, and that's how she appeared through the book. Dead-Laura would have been wearing a blue suit.

His phone buzzed. *She was in a navy blue suit with skirt on Friday. Saturday she was in a green pantsuit. Emerald, not kelly or lime. Why is that important in the middle of the night?*

Blue. Powersuit. That was the connection between the two seemingly-random poisonings; both victims had been wearing blue suits on Friday. By Saturday, when Valerie had died, the connection had vanished, but it had been there on Friday.

And there was the motivation for Tasha/Dead-Laura's death — it had been a mistake. The murderer had intended to kill Valerie.

Jacob closed the tab and turned slowly back to Christopher and Mickey. The poison had been meant for Valerie and had gone to the wrong person, but it hadn't gone to just any wrong person. Someone had gotten directions to put the powder into Valerie's food, and no one had supposed there would be two women in blue suits at a con, where business dress was decidedly out of the usual.

That meant there were two murderers, or at least a murderer and an uncomprehending accomplice who had access to the victims' food. Someone like a kitchen worker, or a fast food employee....

Oh.

He looked up to see Christopher staring hard at Mickey. "You don't get it, man. I put a lot into that show."

"A lot of money?" Jacob asked quietly.

Christopher looked at him. "Well, yeah."

Something else clicked for Jacob. "Did you produce episodes already? Did you hire Rick Yoshinaga?"

Christopher's eyebrows lowered. "Yes, I did. I did a whole season, once FunFilms gave me the go-ahead. We rented a studio, built sets, got lights, the whole works. It looks fabulous! Not that anyone's going to see it."

"You could release it online yourself," Mickey said.

Christopher snorted. "It's never going to recoup the cost that went into it. Even if it got decent ad revenues, I'm still going to have to declare bankruptcy. Rick's in trouble too, since you already know about him. I was going to pay him out of what FunFilms and then MEGAN!ME were supposed to pay me."

"And since Valerie shut down your show before you got paid," Jacob said, "you needed her out of the way so you could try to get it back again."

Christopher seemed to go still. "I just said I wondered if that would happen now, yes."

Mickey's mouth opened, but it was a second or so before he spoke. "Oh, no. Christopher."

Christopher looked between them, and then he seemed to decide. "I came by after you tweeted about the conservatory photos, just to see what exactly you were looking for. The fact that you didn't mention me in them got me worried." He drew a box-cutter from his pocket and extended the blade. "That's not the kind of thing you leave out unless you think you might be talking to a murderer."

"It wasn't like that," Jacob said. The metal chair seemed very tight against his back. The pass-through was open, and if they shouted someone down in the lobby might hear, but that wouldn't save them. At best, someone would call police to confirm that yes, they'd been murdered in the same way the zombie had been.

Christopher couldn't reach them both. He had to decide which of them to attack first.

"And then you were kind enough to explain that this

was your suspicion and not the police line. And it's an easy enough thing to explain away, now that Ken isn't talking."

"Ken is the Fierce Burger zombie," Jacob said numbly. His phone was still in his hand, resting on the chair by his leg.

"'Fierce Burger zombie' isn't a phrase you get to say very often," Christopher mused. "But yes, you're right."

Mickey took a step forward. "Christopher, you can't—"

Christopher swung toward him, the box-cutter extended. "Don't move!"

Jacob slid the touch-lock on his phone and glanced down at the keyboard which appeared beneath his thumb. He thumbed *911* and hit *Send* just as Christopher whirled back. "What are you doing?"

Jacob leaned back as Christopher reached forward with the box-cutter and snatched the phone with the other hand. "What did you do? Who did you call?"

"No one," Jacob answered. "I didn't call anyone."

Christopher looked at the screen. "You texted 911? Seriously? Not even *to* 911?"

The phone had unlocked to the text conversation with Sam, of course. Jacob's heart sank.

Christopher hit the call button, dialing Sam. "I'm going to tell her that if she calls I'll kill — busy signal? Your girlfriend's quick, isn't she." He looked at Jacob. "Oh, right, not your girlfriend."

Good, Sam. Jacob exhaled, his breath tight in his chest. Now they just had to survive until the police arrived.

That was often harder than it sounded.

"Is that what you used to kill that Ken guy?" Mickey said.

Christopher shook his head. "Don't be stupid. That went in a trash can behind the hotel hours ago. The nice thing about sharp stuff, though, is that it's everywhere. So easy to come by, and nobody ever tracks it."

Mickey looked at Jacob and then back at Christopher. "Christopher, this is stupid. Three people are dead. You can't kill two more."

"It was supposed to be just one," he said. "Just Valerie, and really who would miss her? But stupid Ken gave the stuff to the wrong woman."

Keep him talking. "What did Ken have against her?" Jacob asked. "What had she done to him?" He made the question serious, not indignant. Let Christopher rant and rage and burn time until the police could arrive.

"He didn't," Christopher said. "He thought it was something else. He was happy to help out a celebrity. I told him she was my girlfriend, and we'd had a fight, and it was just something to help her be, you know, more friendly. More cooperative."

"I can't imagine why your girlfriend is now an ex-girlfriend," Mickey said dryly.

Christopher jerked toward him and then caught himself as Jacob shifted in his chair, swinging the box-cutter toward him again. "Oh, no. You stay put."

Jacob raised his hands, both conceding to Christopher and warning Mickey to stay where he was. Knives were as dangerous as guns — sometimes more so. A gunshot made a single hole, while a knife slash could open long wounds which bled free and fast. There was a reason police were trained to confront and, if necessary, shoot hostile knife-wielders from a distance.

They were close, and Jacob had no gun.

"But Ken caught on after Tasha was found dead."

"Was that her name? Yeah, but not right away. It wasn't supposed to be obvious, not for a while, and by the time anyone started thinking murder we'd be getting out of here. And I figured he'd be the type to keep his mouth shut rather than admit he'd helped. Even if he didn't think it was poison, date rape drugs aren't the kind of attention he'd want, either."

He paused, and Jacob tensed. He had to keep him talking. "But he got chicken."

"He kind of put it together after Valerie died."

"And Ken realized he wasn't accessory to make-up rape, but to murder."

"He came to me, wanted to talk. Of course that's not the kind of thing you can talk about. I told him I'd get more money for him, he wasn't sure if he wanted to go for it, but he came back to pick it up anyway. Greedy bastard was probably going to take my money and then rat me out."

"He came right before the zombie crawl?"

"I told him it would be a good way to not be identified, in case anyone saw him."

It was a foolishly antagonistic thing to say, but Jacob couldn't stop himself. "And you let him panic and bleed out in the middle of hundreds of clueless people who didn't know to help him. That's sick. Really sick."

"You think I wanted that? It wasn't my idea. But look at what kind of person he was — he was fine with taking money to help me drug a ho. I just wanted to get rid of someone no one would be sorry about. Everyone would talk about how they were horrified but they'd all be secretly glad she was gone, and I figured people wouldn't even stress about helping police too much because they'd all be kind of relieved, if anyone even thought it wasn't some sort of accident. That's all I wanted, and he was the one who was drugging girls and then trying to scam me while he went behind my back. He got what he deserved."

"And what about Tasha?" asked Mickey. "What did she deserve? She was a fan, Christopher, same as you. And you murdered her and two other people. I hope you fry."

"Shut up," snarled Christopher. He glanced between them, realizing he was wasting time he didn't have, if Sam had indeed called the police.

Mickey read it too. "You can't take us both," he said. "You caught Ken off-guard, I'll bet, but you can't surprise us and you can't take both of us at once. Drop the knife."

"Mickey," Jacob cautioned.

But the voice actor shifted his weight. "Come on, Jacob. Together we can take him, hold him for the police. Let's—"

Christopher lunged, catching Mickey's upflung arm with one hand and slashing with the other. The box cutter carved a red streak across Mickey's face. Jacob hit Christopher's back as its second stroke swept across Mickey's neck, catching in his throat.

Christopher spun with a roar and Jacob ducked, the blade scorching hot across his upper arm. He scrabbled backward — *charge the gun, flee the knife* — and scanned desperately for something he could use as a shield or weapon.

Christopher lunged, and Jacob caught the metal folding chair and swung it hard. Christopher yelped and swore as it struck his arm, but it wasn't the hand which held the box-cutter, and he stumbled over the chair and came on.

Jacob seized one side of the table and heaved, overturning it in Christopher's path. Jacob bolted, tripping over the computer's power cord which snapped taut, and slid across the multi-colored industrial carpet.

Christopher kicked aside the falling computer and climbed over the table. Jacob scrambled forward, beneath the skirted table along the wall, where at least Christopher would have to crouch or move furniture to reach him. He bumped into a plastic bin and squeezed past it, and then he realized what it was.

"I'll kill you!" Christopher snarled. "You won't get a chance to tell them what you think you know!"

Jacob reached an arm between the edge of the bin and the loose lid and grasped. *Please. Oh, God, please.* He lifted the first and discarded it, but the second was plausible.

Christopher hurled the table to one side and then recoiled as Jacob rolled and sighted the gun on him. "Back off," Jacob ordered, his voice shaking. "Now."

Christopher hesitated. "Where'd that come from? You can't carry a weapon at the con."

"No, but we can stash one for emergencies. This is Con Ops, we have money and stuff here. It seemed like a good idea, what with the killings and all." Jacob shifted his weight slowly, rolling upright.

Christopher didn't move. "You're bluffing."

"Try me, then. You know what I am, what I've been training to be. You know I'm prepared to shoot if necessary. And I just watched you cut an innocent and unarmed man, so it'd be pretty easy to argue it was necessary." How long could he keep this up? How long before the police arrived, before Christopher realized the truth? "Mickey? You okay over there?"

There was a sickly croak from the far side of the office.

Jacob didn't take his eyes from Christopher. "You hang in there, Mickey. Help is on the way. Just hang on."

Christopher took a breath, but it was unsteady. "I can't let you tell them."

"They have all the same pictures," Jacob said. "It's only a matter of time. And I already texted Daniel to ask if the zombie was the Fierce Burger guy, and they'll have him identified by tomorrow, even without me mentioning it. And then they'll put it together with the photos. It's already over, Christopher, you just haven't caught on yet. There's nothing you can do about it — nothing you could do at all, once you killed them. It's over."

His shoulder was burning and his shirt felt wet. He didn't look away from Christopher. "It might not have been me," Christopher said. "It might have been someone cosplaying me. That happens. I'm famous, people know me. It might have been someone playing me." But it sounded desperate, and his expression was all despair and panic.

That panic worried Jacob. "Give it up," he said, trying with only moderate success to keep his voice steady. "It'll only get worse if you keep going. Give it up."

Christopher swallowed visibly. "Ken can't tell them anything, and no one can connect his powder to me. The photos aren't conclusive. I just have to shut you up." His voice was rising, as if he were trying to steel himself to rush the gun.

"Christopher, don't," Jacob said.

And then Christopher's eyes widened. "That's one of the confiscated fake gun props, isn't it?"

Jacob tried to remain still, but Christopher saw something to confirm his guess. He extended the box cutter and rushed forward.

Jacob jerked upward, trying to get to his feet while keeping the fake gun in front of him. The gun barrel took the first slash of the cutter, catching it against the plastic trigger guard which snapped with the impact. Christopher grabbed the gun and Jacob released it, recoiling and knowing that he couldn't stumble backward fast enough to avoid the cutter's next sweep.

"Get down!"

A pole stabbed over Jacob's shoulder and struck Christopher just below the collarbone, shoving him hard. He fell backward, folding a little and grasping at his chest. "What—"

Jacob looked up and back and saw Sam slide across the pass-through counter, one hand holding the glaive and the other springboarding her over Jacob and into the Con Ops office. "Back off."

Christopher's face twisted, and he snarled something deeply misogynistic. He started forward, hand and box cutter extended.

Sam swung the glaive, using not just her arms but her full body, and cracked the staff across his shoulder. The pole splintered, snapping in half where the two pieces joined, and Christopher stumbled but did not go down. Sam gripped the remaining part of her staff, stepped forward and reversed direction, catching his head this time.

The hollow crack made Jacob flinch despite himself. Christopher went to one knee, wavering but still upright. Sam glanced over her shoulder to where Mickey had been, out of Jacob's sight now beyond the upturned table. Without speaking she turned back and raised the staff high, striking downward as if splitting wood, and the bones of Christopher's knife wrist broke audibly.

He screamed and dropped the box cutter, clutching at his arm with his other hand. Jacob rolled to his feet. "Sam? You okay?"

"Why wouldn't I be?" She took a step and kicked the box cutter away from where Christopher had dropped it. "Keep an eye on that, or whatever you do."

The door was open, Jacob realized, and Lydia was kneeling beside Mickey. Jacob grabbed a sheet of printer paper and picked up the box cutter — no fingerprints, keep control of the weapon — and then went to where Lydia was pressing hard against Mickey's throat.

Oh, no. Not again. Not again. Jacob grabbed a Con Aid shirt from the dwindling supply and pushed it against the bloody wound, Lydia's fingers closing on it and holding it tight. "Hang on, Mickey, help's coming."

Christopher swore and lunged at Sam, who jumped backward and swung the staff with less precision. Still the blow caught him in the head again, and he went down slowly and unsteadily, sitting upright but loose on the floor.

Jacob's mind reeled. He couldn't do much more to help Mickey; Lydia had pressure on the wound, and that was all they could offer at the moment. Securing Christopher was next, but he didn't have cuffs or a weapon. Where was the other half of Sam's glaive?

"How is he?" Sam called without looking.

He couldn't answer her without scaring Mickey further, and Mickey needed to stay calm — or as calm as possible, anyway. "He'll be okay. Help's coming soon."

"Help's here," Lydia said, as figures came in the door, guns and cuffs in hand.

Chapter Thirty One

"Christopher Adams," said Daniel slowly, testing the consonants. "Yeah, I guess it's there. R-F-D."

Sam and Jessica sat on either side of Jacob, with Zach nearby. Sam had an arm around him, carefully below the line of stitches across his upper arm and shoulder. Daniel sat on the edge of a table, a few empty cups of ramen discarded behind him, and Detective Martin was seated near him. Vince was also in the staff suite, looked haggard but faintly relieved.

"It was the *chibi* after all." Detective Martin shook her head. "I've lived too long, to see the day a man kills over a big-eyed cutesy mascot."

"And bankruptcy," added Daniel. "He spent a lot to produce that show. He expected to get his investment back."

"And he has a history — unofficially — of violence against women," Detective Martin added darkly. "Been arrested three times for domestic, but neither woman would testify against him and charges were dropped. So this isn't such a surprise. Just an escalation."

"He'd been arrested before?" Sam repeated.

"But without testimony, they probably couldn't get a conviction," Jacob explained.

"Yeah," Jessica said, "but maybe three more people would be alive today."

There was a moment of chill silence, and then Daniel rose from the corner of the table. "Only three," he said. "Mickey's going to be okay. They're not positive how his voice will be, but the doctors say he's got a really good chance."

"I ought to go and see him," Jacob said. "He probably saved my life. If Christopher hadn't been torn between us, he would have been cutting me wholesale. I'd never have had time to text Sam or get to the confiscated guns."

"Oh, about that." Daniel nodded toward Jacob. "That's assault."

"What?"

"Pointing a fake gun at someone. Assault." He shrugged. "But in this case it was pretty clearly self-defense, so no arrest will be made."

Jacob grinned, but Sam did not. "Are you kidding me? For a fake gun?"

"It's not about whether the gun is real," Daniel said. "It's about how it's used. And yep, lots of cases of felonies with fake or unloaded guns."

"Well, Jacob's a hero," she said with an edged voice.

"Stand down, Sam. He's just razzing me."

"Still. Seems like maybe people would be more concerned about the real murderers."

"We are," said Detective Martin sharply, "or hadn't you noticed?" She gave a little jerk of her head toward the Con Ops room, where a few technicians were still marking blood spatters and evidence. "Adams has been arrested and is in jail awaiting a public defender, as he says he can't afford one of his own."

"Relax, Sam," Jacob said. "What he says is true, but it's also true that I wouldn't be convicted for using a toy gun against a murderer who had just knifed someone."

That much was true; it had been pretty undeniably self-defense. But what if Daniel were giving him a subtle hint about the Academy? Would they maybe look unfavorably on an applicant who had pulled a toy gun, especially if that applicant had a dubious psychological background of reality television dysfunction?

"And we have a confirmed sighting of him in the hotel bar this morning — yesterday morning — what time is it, anyway?" Detective Martin shook her head. "No, don't tell me, I'd only fall asleep. Anyway, he was seen going into the bar where Valerie was waiting, since someone told her Vince would meet her there."

Jacob felt a sudden stab of guilt.

"So that's when he must have gone in to argue with her. It's possible he was trying to talk her one last time into picking up his show, but since he'd already arranged the first poisoning, it's more likely it was just a cover to get close to whatever she was drinking."

"He must have been surprised to see her when he came into Con Ops that morning," Daniel said. "He probably wanted to confirm that there'd been a death the night before, but then there she was, alive as ever and even insulting him."

"And I sent her away," said Jacob. "I told her to wait in the bar for Vince."

Daniel looked at him. "Don't feel any guilt about that," he said. "Well, a little, for yanking her chain, but you were just trying to get her off Vince's back. You weren't responsible for what happened. Christopher Adams killed three people, attacked and robbed Laser, and tried to kill two more. He would have gone after Valerie regardless of anything you did."

Jacob nodded, and Sam gave him a little squeeze.

"So let all that be on Christopher's head, not yours."

Jacob swallowed. "What about the Academy?"

"What?"

Jacob blew out his breath. "It'll be bad publicity if I go ahead with my application, right? Little Jakey to serve and protect? So I guess...." He didn't want to finish the sentence.

"It will be bad publicity, all right," replied Detective Martin coolly. "A police science major works out a homicide case, is attacked by the murderer, holds him off with a toy until help can arrive for the injured victim, and then the Academy turns him down? Yeah, that's the kind of publicity we certainly can't afford. Very bad." She stood. "Just don't get a big head, or it'll turn into a chip on your shoulder for everyone to knock off."

Jacob stared at her a moment. "You mean, you think they'll take me?"

"I've been wrong before, but I'd be willing to play some money on this one." She smiled. "See you soon, Jacob Tarston Foster."

She rose and went to the door, but as she opened it she stopped.

Daniel jerked to his feet. "What?"

"Not bad," she answered immediately. "Just — weird."

They all went to the door and looked down to the lobby, where a group was dancing to a small set of speakers blasting Britney Spears' "Hit Me Baby One More Time," slightly overdriven. They were dressed in what could only be described as trailer park chic — a too-tight pink knit dress with a leopard-print jacket and over-sized plastic earrings, a stained wife-beater beneath an open plaid shirt, a Hooters t-shirt. There were perhaps a dozen of them, the women in teased wigs of bleached blonde or a red never found in nature and the men in mullets. One man had pulled his shirt high, just covering his nipples in accordance with the hotel's dress code, and was using both hands to jiggle his ample belly in time with the music. Fake cigarettes dangled from nearly every lip.

"What in the world is that?" asked Jessica. "Really, what?"

Jacob's stomach dropped hard and fast, and he tasted bile. Sam put an arm around his shoulders, but she had nothing to say.

People were gathered around the dancers, laughing and taking photos as they pretended to drink from red party cups and then staggered through their moves or pushed one another angrily. Jacob saw one thin cosplayer in a striped shirt — they must have made it themselves, surely no one still sold anything that ugly — bend and, with a quick movement that felt like a punch to Jacob's stomach, jerked down his pants to expose flesh-toned leggings and waggled his butt at one of the bleached blondes.

Sam elbowed Jessica. "It's everyone from *Cougars and Cold Ones*. The whole cast. Somebody actually wanted to cosplay *Cougars and Cold Ones*."

Jessica tilted her head. "I can't decide whether to be happy Jacob's so famous or go punch them for being insensitive."

"Don't," Jacob started, but Jessica had already started forward.

"She ain't happy unless she's righting a wrong," Sam sighed, and she started after her. Jacob followed.

Jessica's voice carried over the straining speakers. "Turn that off! Do you guys have any idea how—"

"It's him!" shrieked one of the bleached blondes. "It's Jakey!"

They rushed, and Jacob froze. And then they were around him, all talking at once, and someone pushed next to him and held up a phone for a selfie.

Sam wedged herself between them. "A little space, please?"

"Hold on," Jacob managed. "What's going on?"

The guy playing Little Jakey — playing Jacob — worked his way to the front. "We've been planning this for weeks, you know? Wanted to put together a whole group. We've got the whole cast, worked out all our choreography, all of it. We had no idea you'd be here!"

"That was you guys, wasn't it?" Sam's eyes widened. "You were the ones sneaking *Cougars* into all the viewing rooms and everywhere?"

Little Jakey grinned. "Yeah! We thought it'd be fun to get everyone buzzed before we made our big appearance on Sunday. Cool, right?"

"Do a photo with us?" asked the redhead dressed like his Aunt Ginnie. "Please? A big group shot?"

"Yes, please?" That was from the one he supposed was his mother. It was disorienting and disconcerting.

But they looked so eager and hopeful and not at all mocking. They were playing with the personalities, not attacking them.

"Um," Jacob said, "sure."

They lined up around him, striking various signature poses — including the classic pants-down — and cameras flashed all about the lobby. Jacob's face burned, and he wondered if he should have refused. There was no going back now.

His eyes found Sam's in the watching crowd, and she gave him a small smile. It would be okay.

Beside her, Jessica was taking a photo, too.

The group around him changed poses frequently, milking photos from the laughing spectators, but after a few moments they began to break apart. "Thanks, man," said Little Jakey to Jacob. "You made my day. Week. Month."

"Yeah, thank you," said his faux-mother. "We were just hoping someone would recognize us by Sunday. This was awesome."

Jacob nodded. "Glad you enjoyed it." And he was, he found. He wasn't sure yet if he'd enjoyed it, but he wasn't as angry with them as he would have thought.

"Food," Sam said. "Real food. Eggs and fruit and stuff. Food trucks are here, so come on."

"Coming."

His phone buzzed, and he glanced down at a text from Lydia. It was only a smiley face and a bit.ly link. He clicked, and it opened to a tweet from the Herald.

Child reality star, now hero, Jakey Tarston saves actor's life, holds alleged knife-wielding assailant 'til police arrive. Story developing.

Story developing. That was a nice way to put it. Not like he'd planned, not at all, but story developing.

He let Sam and Jessica pull him toward the food trucks.

Did you enjoy *Con Job*? Please leave a review! It's one of the best things you can do for a book, and I do read every one. Thank you!

About the Author

Laura VanArendonk Baugh is a behavior expert, animal trainer, and chocolate enthusiast who has attended and worked at quite a lot of anime, sci-fi, comic, gaming, and other conventions. She's won about thirty costume awards at cons ranging in size from a few hundred to over fifty thousand attendees, judged costume contests, and presented well over one hundred workshops on costuming, fandom, and related topics – so she enjoyed this chance to get her geek on in fiction as well.

www.LauraVanArendonkBaugh.com
www.AndSewingIsHalfTheBattle.com

Laura's other titles include:
Kitsune-Tsuki
Kitsune-Mochi

Smoke and Fears
Smoke and Peers

Fired Up, Frantic, and Freaked Out:
Training Crazy Dogs from Over-the-Top to Under Control

and a variety of short stories

Remember WENN

"Tell us how you escaped from Devil's Island, Randolph."

"Oh, Doug, I'm far too busy to be upset. I have my broadcasts, my fan mail, my detailed plans for how to dispose of Jeff's body...."

These lines from Sam's voice audition are borrowed from *Remember WENN*, a brilliant show which, like *Firefly*, was canceled by management despite its popularity but unlike *Firefly*, never got a DVD release. (Read more on the greatest television series you've never seen at http://lauravanarendonkbaugh.com/remember-wenn/)

The lines were spoken by the inimitable Miss Hilary Booth (played by Melinda Mullins), an actress complaining of poorly-written scripts who finally bursts, "I've even had to say, 'Tell us how you escaped from Devil's Island, Randolph!'" More than fifteen years later, as I was trying to write a flat and terrible line, Hilary's diatribe ran through my mind, and as I knew any pathetic line I tried to write after that would be a pale copy of that perfectly limp phrase, I decided to honor her lost show with that line and the next. Original writing credit goes to show's creator and writer Rupert Holmes. I'd love to give you a link to purchase the DVDs, but....

WENN fans may recognize another audition reference as well, but it's more oblique to keep things spoiler-free.

www.ingramcontent.com/pod-product-compliance
Lightning Source LLC
Chambersburg PA
CBHW020414110726
47899CB00006B/1975